This High School Has Closets

This High School Has Closets

ROBERT JOSEPH GREENE

ICON EMPIRE PRESS
Toronto Vancouver New York London

Published in Canada by
Icon Empire Press
628 – 1755 Robson Street
Vancouver, BC V6G 3B7

Published in the U.S. by
Icon Empire Press
PO Box 1108
Bridgeport,CT 06601-1108

Printed and bound in Canada by Webcom
10 9 8 7 6 5 4 3 2 1

LIBRARY AND ARCHIVES CANADA CATALOGUING IN PUBLICATION

Greene, Robert, 1973–
   This High School Has Closets. English

ISBN 978-1-927124-04-8

1. Gay teenagers--Fiction. I. Title.

PS8613.R435T55 2012   C813'.6   C2012-901251-3

Also issued in electronic format.
ISBN 978-1-927124-12-3

United States Of America Library of Congress Control Number: 2012937959

ACKNOWLEDGEMENTS

I would like to thank Camilla Greene, Thomas Greene, Kelli-Anne, Caleb Greene, Stanley Bennett Clay, Catherine Adamson (a special THANK YOU!), Holly Whu, Robert Windisman, Bobby Nijjar, Dan Mohan, John Weger, Stephanie Yuen, Alexander Hopkins, for their proofreading and editing and/or moral support.

NOTICE

TABLE OF CONTENTS

CHAPTER ONE. A New Student   11

CHAPTER TWO. The Kiss   21

CHAPTER THREE. Basketball   35

CHAPTER FOUR. Barry's House   45

CHAPTER FIVE. The Game   59

CHAPTER SIX. School Dance   63

CHAPTER SEVEN. Breakfast   76

CHAPTER 8. The Mark Hall Story   86

CHAPTER 9. Rave Party   91

CHAPTER 10. After High School   100

A New Student

Abbey Park High isn't much of a modern high school. It's actually a throwback to the 1960's in its design. Abbey Park High is known for its basketball team, a team on which I play second string. For an idea about how tight the competition is, in middle school I was the most valuable player, with a record for most dunks in a season. Now I'm at the bottom of the list. I tell myself that being at the bottom is okay, because most of our players get athletic scholarships from big universities, so maybe I'll get noticed by a few universities myself.

"Mark Thomas, please answer the question." "Oh, I don't know," I reply in exasperation. We both realize that I had been daydreaming and so my fourth period Math teacher, Mr. Sakolosky, repeats the question. "Can you solve the equation and give a value for x?" I gaze up at the board just in time to hear the bell. Saved. I shoot out of there as I hear Mr. Sakolosky shouting out tomorrow's assignments.Walking to my locker, Todd Polino says, "See you at practice." I remind him it's Wednesday, which is a study day. I leave him thinking that he needs the study day more than I. Todd is one of the sexiest guys I have ever seen. He's tall, lean, and fit. He has light brown eyes but dark hair and dimples. I blush at my stupid thoughts. I guess I have thoughts on just about every guy in high school. I wonder when my attention will turn to girls. The school isn't far from home; I can walk but I usually take the bus. The bus is full of first- and second-year geeks who are unusually rowdy. Mine is the third stop. I hop off and see my dog, Taggs, running towards me. He is jumping high enough to lick my face. Taggs jumps in spurts. "Cut it out you stupid dog!" I say while laughing. As I arrive on the doorstep, I lift the mat to get the key. I know mom isn't home yet because her car isn't in the driveway. She's probably showing a home. Mom works in real estate. She didn't work when I was a kid, but now that I'm older she seems to be occupying most of her time working in real estate. I wonder if she regrets having a family.

I throw my books in the foyer and head for the kitchen. I pour myself a glass of milk and grab some Pop-Tarts. I know mom would disapprove of my avoiding the healthy apples and oranges in the bowl on the table, but that's the advantage of having a working mom. I can now enjoy one of my many secret pleasures when home alone: watching All My Children. After the show finishes, I snooze a bit on the couch, dreaming about Todd Polino, Hollis Nordstrom and other guys on the team running up and down the court. I wake up to keys jingling in the lock. It's mom, arriving with a load of groceries. I know that there are more bags so I scurry to help her.

Mom and dad divorced when I was twelve. Dad lives in Kitchener, about a two-and-a-half-hour drive from our suburban home. We never talk much about it but they seem to be okay. Dad's remarried and has a four-year-old daughter named Heather. I don't see her much but dad comes to every one of my games.

Little is said between us as I help mom unpack the bags. She orders pizza for dinner. We eat in silence and then I go upstairs to do my homework and go to bed. The rest of the week is uneventful until the following Wednesday. I decide to take a brisk walk to school. I am a bit of a morning person and like watching the morning unfold as I begin my day's journey.

When I arrive at homeroom, I notice that the once vacant seat next to mine is taken. Its new occupant is none other than a player from Markham District High's basketball team. Markham District High School is our rival school, situated north of Toronto. Last year, our two teams were in the basketball finals and had a near riot during the game. The guy occupying the seat quickly eyes me, but says nothing. He seems cool and mellow. Our principal starts the morning announcements over the PA system. We then sit down and

Mrs. Sturbridge, our homeroom teacher, approaches our newest addition to review his schedule. I glance at his card from across the desk. I can't really focus on which classes he has because Mrs. Sturbridge is in my way. As I strain to get a better look, he glances my way and I blush at getting caught being so nosey. To make matters even worse, Mrs. Sturbridge turns to me with his card in her hand and asks if I have any of these classes. With the card in full view, I see his name: Barry Stillwater. We share four out of seven classes, including first period. I tell Mrs. Sturbridge that I will take him to his next class. Realizing that this just exposed them to the fact that I was snooping, I want to crawl under my seat in embarrassment. Mrs. Sturbridge feels it is her cue to introduce us and I blush as I mumble my name, which is almost inaudible. "Speak up," said Mrs. Sturbridge, "even I can't hear you." The whole class giggles and I blush some more because this is now the highlight of homeroom and all heads are turned our way. "Mark Thomas," I repeat. "Good. You're in good hands, Barry," she says as she returns to her desk. Martha Beland shapes her hands like the Allstate Insurance commercial representing "good hands" which makes the class laugh even louder. In this moment I could have died from embarrassment. I don't dare look at Barry as I can imagine he is just as thrilled as I am at the unwanted attention. When the bell rings, he gets up and grabs his books. He waits just outside the homeroom door but doesn't look at me as I'm coming out. He just looks straight ahead. I feel kind of hurt at this gesture, but proceed to strike up a conversation anyway while walking him to our next classroom. I'm known to be a loner, so speaking to other people is really an effort for me. I ask him a lot of dumb questions, like didn't he go to Markham District High, and did they have eight periods or seven? He gives me one word answers or just nods. When we get to class, he doesn't sit next to me, which makes me feel uneasy. It's assigned seating anyway, but he could have made the effort. In fact, he sits right across the classroom by the wall. Our first period class is history. I can't concentrate because I'm thinking about what I could have done wrong. Just then, Principal Andrews comes in and asks that Barry be excused. He never returns to class that day or to the other classes we share. I am able to put him out of my mind until lunchtime when I overhear a conversation by some of the girls in my grade at the table behind me talking about some hot guy in class. Cynthia Tyler even goes on to say that he has the sexiest hairy legs on a man that she's ever seen. I make a mental note to check out Barry's legs next time we have PE.

It is Wednesday and there isn't any practice, so at the end of the day I decide to take the bus home. I notice that Barry is on the same bus but I make it a point not to sit next to him. The third stop is mine and I get off, and to my surprise he follows. "You live on Ashford?" I ask, breaking my promise to myself to be cool around him.

"No, Hemmington," he says as he walks past me.

"How come you weren't in the other classes with me

today? You could have gotten off at the next stop you know." Barry doesn't answer. He walks slowly so that I can catch up. I find myself walking just to say something to him. I pass my house realizing what I am doing without acknowledging it. However, it is noticed by Taggs, who's just about to shoot towards me with his great big jump-and-lick routine, but I think the presence of Barry startles him. "So, why did you move to Oakville?" He doesn't answer; instead, he asks me a question.

"Do you live on Hemmington?"

"No, Ashford," I reply, realizing what a mistake I made because we are at the point where Ashford and Hemmington intersect and there are no more houses on Ashford. I know that I am blushing and quickly change the subject. "So, are you going to play basketball?"

"Yeah, the coaches asked that I come to practice but I don't know if the team is set and all."

"Well, I'm sure there's room for one more," I say, like a complete loser.

"It's kind of cold so I'm heading in . . . see ya." Barry turns to go up Hemmington.

I walk back to my house nearly 500 feet from where I leave Barry. I hope that he doesn't turn back to see how far I walked just to talk to him. Taggs trots alongside me as I enter the driveway. I think dogs can sense our moods. Mom's car is in the driveway. She must not have had any showings this evening. When I get in, I feel kind of depressed, figuring how desperate I must have looked to Barry, following him and all. When I enter the house the lights are on and music is playing from a clock radio in the kitchen. I have to admit it's nice to come home when someone else is here. Taggs gallops into the kitchen to see if he can get some scraps of food to eat. I don't bother to say hi. I just drop my coat and book bag and go up to my room.

Mom yells at me, "Mark, do you feel like Chinese tonight?"

"Yeah," I call back. I sit there wondering when the last time was that she made a meal in this house. She knocks on my door.

"Can I come in?"

"Enter," I grunt. She tells me she closed on two houses. That is a relief because I know she has been worrying. She tells me that one of the houses she sold last month is just around the corner. Apparently she befriended the lady and tells me that she has three children and one of them is my age. My heart is just about to sink. "Their last name wouldn't be Stillwater, would it?"

"Why yes; do you know their kid?" she asks inquisitively with a smile on her face.

"He's a boy, and his name is Barry," I add but she isn't listening anymore. She is going through her cell phone, scrolling for the Chinese restaurant's number. "Whatever." The next day, I don't have much time to speak to Barry because we are both rushing for the bus. During our morning classes, he doesn't pay any attention to me and I am resigned to this being the norm. By lunchtime, I have pretty much gotten through over-analyzing everything and daydreaming through my classes. I'm a good student but lately I'd been preoccupied. The lunch bell rings and I bolt to the lunch line for hot lunches. Spaghetti or a version of it is always on the menu. I sit in my usual spot just behind "the girls" as I call them. Their gossip, which I publicly criticize as being very childish and petty, tends to play as entertainment through lunch. The lunchroom, like all high school lunch rooms, has a section for all the various school cliques: goths, freaks, cheerleaders, jocks, and even the band has its own groupie section. My seat, like I say, is just behind "the girls." It is sort of a mismatched group of people who sit at this table and everyone wonders why I sit there, rather than with the jocks or some other "guys" group. Only I know the truth: it's fun listening to their chatter. As I ease into my seat, I notice Barry coming towards me. I look away in order to act surprised. I can feel my heart pounding in anticipation.

"Hey," he says as he slides into the seat across from me. I know that all the girls' eyes are on us as they gleam for new gossip on the wonder kid that is Barry. He just sits there and starts eating. That is all. No words. No conversation. I am frustrated and decide to start a dialogue once again. "Is the food as bad at Markham District?" I ask. He chuckles and says it's much worse but goes on to explain that they did have more options. As he continues to talk I think to myself: This is more than I have heard from him since I met him. I'm happy to finally be having a real conversation with him.

He asks if I am going to practice. I don't remember my telling him that I was on the team. I say, "Yes, I am." He tells me that he will be at practice too. It is then that I realize that he will probably be in the first string and we wouldn't be on the same play schedules. First string practices separately on the real court, the one with the bleachers. Second string gets the multi-purpose gym. My heart sinks as I realize that he will know that I am not as good a player. This is bad because then he'll realize that 1st string and 2nd string players don't mix. We speak some more about the differences between the Markham District and Abbey Park teams and the play strategies. I speak as if I know something about the 1st string when I really don't.

Todd Polino comes and sits with us. A tinge of jealousy strikes me, listening to the ease of their conversation. I feel like the odd man out and struggle to participate in the conversation. Todd is on 1st string. He is also known as the Don Juan of Abbey Park High. He has a steady girlfriend, Judy Aronson, and is reported to have gone all the way with her. Judy denies the rumour. Judy has somehow convinced herself that since she and Todd are getting married after high school she doesn't have to bother with the "nonsense" of getting good grades. Todd asks Barry if he knows Rick Porter from Markham District High. Barry says he does. Todd goes on to say that he is his cousin. They continue to talk, ignoring me. It is obvious that Todd isn't here to talk to me even though

I've sat here all year. So I eat in silence and listen to their conversation. My eyes dart everywhere, trying not to seem like I'm staring at Barry. I settle on staring at his shoes. It is innocent enough and a safe place to rest my eyes. I notice he is wearing VANS. They are in gorgeous black suede and are either new or exceptionally clean. I am done with lunch and decide the cool thing to do would be to leave them like I don't care. "See you guys," I say, and walk off. I'm really feeling good for some reason.

CHAPTER TWO

The Kiss

Practice isn't as bad as I think it's going to be. I'm not known as a great player compared to the others, but good enough I suppose. In middle school I was really something, and I'm sure it was my reputation that had something to do with my barely making the grade and getting on 2nd string. Coach Murray often visits the school games to scout for the next year. I was really the class jock back then, but now I'm lucky if I sink one in during practice. The 2nd string guys really have it bad. We get the poorer gym, and while Coach Murray reviews the practice and play strategies, he never remains to watch us go over them. He leaves it up to our lead captain, Mark Macelli, who couldn't care less if we do them or not. I always feel uncomfortable around the other guys. It's been this way since I started playing in high school. The first thing I noticed was that these guys have hair like my dad. I am a bit late in the development of pubic hair, and this makes me self-conscious when changing in front of anyone. I finally grew some over the past few months. This uneasy feeling might have been why I played so poorly this year.Most of the time, we play a few games and keep score. I never know if Mark relays how well we play, or even the score, to Coach Murray. However, today I'm really playing well. I mean I'm actually running circles around everyone and making almost every shot. It is so obvious that Macelli laughs out loud. "What's with you, dude?" he yells. Everyone joins in the laughter, including myself. We play three games and then hit the showers. Everyone is laughing and teasing me. They are asking me what wonder drug made me an all-star all of a sudden. I laugh with them and try to prolong their interest in teasing me back to the change room, hoping that Barry will see my newfound popularity as a good player. There is only one change room, so we share. Unfortunately, Barry is nowhere to be found. I quickly shower and change and go to the main gym where I see him.

Barry is all alone shooting hoops. He doesn't see me watching him from the doorway. It is the first time I really get a good look at him. He is a little taller than me. His hair is very thick and wavy, almost curly. I remember my mother once showing me a box for a hair-coloring kit. The model on the box had hair just like Barry's color. I remember the box saying Auburn Brown. His hair is really thick with big tuffs everywhere, but short enough so that it doesn't get in the way. Barry's physique is solid with well-defined muscles. He is wearing long track pants, which disappoints me. I want to see his legs. His luxuriously hairy legs, as rumour has it. His eyes are a piercing, silver-grey. Sometimes, I'm afraid when he looks at me. His look is so serious and those eyes so startling. I often wonder if he is looking right through me. It is like he can see inside my soul. He has somewhat pale skin, or at least paler than mine. It's funny because I never really considered skin tones until that moment. I don't want to interrupt him. Actually, I want to ask him another one of my lame questions like, why is he staying late, but I know he'll ignore the question. I am feeling more confident . . . a little too confident, because I end up inviting Barry over to shoot a few hoops after practice tomorrow. I guess it startles him too, by the look on his face. I realize that I didn't say hi or anything. I'm sure he is wondering where I came from or for how long I'd been standing there. He thinks about my question for a bit, which annoys me. It is a simple question. He calmly dribbles the ball. At this point all my confidence is gone and I am waiting on his every action, waiting for his answer. I am almost praying for him to reply. Barry stops playing with the ball and slowly walks over to me. He says yes in a distant sort of way like he is preoccupied with something or some thought, and then adds he will be over tomorrow around 4:30, as he exits for the showers. I just stand there. I want to cry. I don't know why I feel really low at this moment.

The gym is quiet. In the background someone is showering in the change room. I know I should have felt excited about getting the answer I wanted, but instead I felt despair and self-hatred.

The next day at school is just a blur. I am glad, though. I was afraid that the day would drag on—as it does when I'm waiting for something to happen—but that wasn't the case today. When the last bell rings, signaling school is over, I bolt to my locker, get my homework and run home. I don't bother taking the bus because I don't want to ruin my meeting with Barry. The excitement might overwhelm him. He might change his mind. Still sweating and slightly tired from the run, I bolt into the foyer, down the stairs and into the garage. I grab a broom and sweep the driveway. The hoop hangs over the garage, like at most homes. When I'm done sweeping I tie Taggs up. Taggs hates being tied up. I've only done it once before, during a barbecue mom was throwing for her co-workers. He nearly choked himself to death that day. At the barbeque, I didn't enjoy myself either, mainly because I hated being around grownups, and of course, I was worried about Taggs. This time Taggs whimpers as if wondering what he did wrong.By the time I'm finished sweeping it's already 4:30. I look nervously up the street only to see it empty. I feel anxious because I don't know what to do with myself. I go and untie Taggs and start playing with him. I rub his belly and we wrestle on the ground. In the corner of my eye, I see a distant figure. My heart starts beating fast when I think that it might be Barry. When I'm sure it's him, I get up, trying to play it cool, and without turning around I start shooting some hoops. I am attempting to show off my talent when he approaches and says hi. My mouth drops. He is wearing a cut-off shirt and I can see a thin string of very fine hair running down his washboard stomach. He has on a pair of really fancy sweats with snaps on the side. The bottom three snaps are undone in a cool sort of way, revealing the much talked about hairy legs. I quickly throw him the ball so that he won't notice me looking at him. We start to shoot a few hoops. The difference in our playing ability is obvious. Barry has no problem running circles around me. Taggs' constant barking makes us stop. "Hey there, fella," Barry says as he wanders over to Taggs, leaving me alone on the court. "Can I take him off the leash," he asks.

"We won't be able to play," I reply, feeling somewhat disappointed in his loss of interest in the game.

"That's okay, I'm kind of tired anyway." Taggs knows that this guy is his savior, and once freed he lunges right at Barry's face to give him a big juicy lick. Barry seems genuinely pleased. "What a great dog," he says. "My mom's allergic to all house pets so we never had a dog or cat." Taggs loves to fetch, so I search for a stick to throw. I find the perfect stick and toss it real easy for Taggs. Taggs runs straight to it and comes back to lay it at my feet. I pass the stick to Barry who lobs it out into the neighbor's yard. At this point, I notice that Barry is smiling. And he has a great smile. It makes him look older than he is.

It isn't long before my mom pulls into the driveway. As she gets out of the car, she looks politely at Barry and asks, "Who's your friend?" I mumble, "Barry Stillwater." As she extends her hand to shake his she comments that we have to have Barry over more often if it makes me clean the driveway without being asked. I am thoroughly embarrassed. She introduces herself as Mrs. Thomas, Mark's mom. Barry shyly replies likewise with his own introduction. "Oh, I sold your parents their house. Well, I'm sure you'll be over more often now that you're our neighbor." At this point I want to crawl under a rock and die. It makes me sound like some desperate loner whose mom has to beg someone to be my friend. We both mumble something of a commitment when Barry says he has to go. Great mom, I think, you scared him off! He quickly trots down the street. Taggs and I watch as Barry's figure shrinks in the distance, as if we just lost a great hero or something. The next day, Barry is waiting at the bus stop with Monica Llewellyn. She is probably one of the prettiest girls in our high school. She is giggling and talking real low with Barry until I arrive. She says hi, and I don't think I ever remember her acknowledging me before, ever. I say hi back, then turn and walk away from them, hoping Barry will follow, but he doesn't. Barry just keeps talking to Monica. I think it's odd that they are at this bus stop, since they have their own stop on Hemmington. Now that I think about it, Monica and Barry are neighbors. Their homes are newer than the homes on my street. I believe the Stillwater's is a four-bedroom colonial. I remember overhearing mom using that as a sales pitch when describing the listing to an interested party over the phone. The bus arrives. When I get on I quickly look for a seat, but all of them are taken. I soon notice two empty aisle seats across from one another. Barry follows me and I am happy that he does. We speak about practice and how mothers can be difficult. The ride is short but meaningful. It starts to feel like Barry is paying me more attention in class. Thump-thump goes my heart.After seventh period, I walk to the gym lockers to change for practice. A bunch of the guys are gathered around Barry like he is some basketball star or something. Although deep in conversation, he manages to look up at me for a moment. When he realizes it's me, he looks away. What, do I have leprosy or something? I ponder my looks for awhile. It's not like I'm unattractive, though I'll admit I probably fall somewhere in the middle where looks are concerned, and I'm not very photogenic. There are hardly any pictures I like of myself. One time while on vacation with my mom at my grandparents' place, we had to dress up for my cousin's graduation. As I was walking out of the auditorium, mom took a photo of me. It's the only picture I have ever liked of myself. I was once asked by this girl, Kathy Bovan, to a dance. We were friends and I was sure she knew that we were going just as friends, but then she cancelled when a better offer came along. Although I understood, I never forgot that moment. So now I think with horror that maybe he knows what I think about guys. I shiver and hope it's not true.

Barry and I take the bus home on a regular basis now. On Friday I'm panicking, hoping that it will stop drizzling, but it doesn't. As we step down off the bus, Taggs thunders towards us at a full run. He jumps all over me. We just stand there. Barry says it's a bummer about the weather. He is about to make his way home and I try to think of a way to keep him from going. "Hey, did you know Taggs can do back flips off the wall?"

"No way," he says, stopping and turning back towards me "Way. Come on, I'll show you." I yell almost too enthusiastically. This is a risky ploy to keep Barry here. For one thing, Taggs doesn't do back flips on cue; he sort of stumbles into it when I am chasing him around the house. The other thing is that mom doesn't like me doing it because Taggs leaves dirty paw prints all over the walls. Anyway, we both go to the front door and I check to see if it's unlocked. Luckily, it isn't. I don't think Barry's been inside my house before. I now examine it critically, as if showing it to an interior decorator. It's outdated in terms of trendy colors and has that well-lived-in look. Barry seems to think nothing of it but I'm embarrassed because it's only a three-bedroom raised ranch, on a smaller property allotment than the Stillwater's. I open the door to let Taggs in and he starts jumping all about. Barry just puts his books down and continues towards the kitchen. The house seems so solemn and empty. I don't want Barry to notice so I turn on lots of lights in the living room, dining room and kitchen. I then turn on the radio. Blur comes on so I crank it up! I offer him some pop but he declines and asks for water. "Tap okay?" He nods yes with that smile that's to die for. I grab Taggs' throw rag and he starts to get excited. More excited than usual. The throw rag is a bunch of shirts tied into knots. It's really soiled and smelly but he doesn't mind. I start to throw it and Taggs goes running after it. Taggs soon realizes it's just a tease and comes back. Barry laughs. I then throw it into the living room. Taggs runs and gets it. Usually, he comes back and leaves it at my foot, but not this time. This time he gives it to Barry who's standing in the archway. Barry smiles and says to Taggs, "You lookin' at me! You lookin' at me?" in his funny Robert de Niro in Taxi Driver accent. We both laugh. Barry takes the rag and throws it in the same direction as the first throw. Taggs is confused because we both call him. He refuses to give the rag to either of us. The next thing I know, Barry and I are chasing Taggs up the stairs and all around the house. Taggs teases us like he wants us to catch him. I am astonished because he has never done this before. I get caught up in the frenzied excitement and am happy to see that Taggs brings it out in Barry as well. We finally corner him under the piano with couch cushions in hand. Mom would have had a coronary at the sight of us using the nice cushions. Both Barry and I dive for Taggs. I fall on the floor and Barry falls too, facing me. Taggs just jumps in between us like he's saying, "Here I am!" Barry and I tickle him while he squirms. Then we're sort of tickling each other. All the while we are laughing hysterically. Taggs darts away, expecting us to dash after him but we don't. The laughter dies down and Barry and I are facing each other. It is awkward. I'm sure we both have every intention to move but I really don't want to. I can feel my heart pounding in my chest. Our breathing is heavy. I've never been so consciously close to Barry before. I feel the tell-tale pressure in my jeans, which makes me embarrassed, although it is hard to tell from my posture that I have an erection. My face blushes at this thought and I feel that something inside of me has been revealed. I shiver from the feel of it, or is it because of my feelings for Barry? I close my eyes for a moment, almost like a long pause, and open them again slowly. Seeing him makes me realize what I am doing. I am about to get up, feeling awkward now, but as my body slowly moves and I position my hand to get up, it slowly falls onto Barry's hand. He moves as if he is trying to steady me, but with no control. I turn my hand inward into his and he holds it. I lean in and kiss Barry very slowly on the lips. But then he kisses me back. His lips are warm and sweet. It dawns on me why they are sweet. Barry must have used cherry flavored lip balm. How odd. As he is kissing me, he puts his hand behind my head and grabs my hair. When he stops kissing me he slowly removes his hand from my hair. It is the silence I first notice, and it all comes crashing down on us as we realize what we just did. We both struggle to get up. I whack the back of my head on the piano as I am trying to stand upright. The piano makes a loud ding and the pain kills me.

"Are you okay?" he asks.

"I'm fine," I lie because I'm seeing stars all around me. We turn away from each other, almost as if we are afraid to look. We half-heartedly laugh and turn our focus onto Taggs, but he has lost interest. I go to throw the rag but there is no effect. Barry laughs at the lame throw and then stops. I close my eyes because I know what he's about to say: Well, I gotta go, it's getting kind of late, or something to that effect. Just then we hear my mom's car pull in. Barry and I look at each other and gasp in paranoia. He grabs his books and flashes mom a quick hello but doesn't stop as he flies out the door.

Mom comes in and immediately notices the couch cushions all over the floor. She proceeds to read me the riot act about how unappreciative I am of her hard work and her few nice things. I am picking up the cushions and not really paying her much attention. I feel like I have a fever. My ears are ringing like I'm having trouble hearing. I am in a daze over what has just happened with Barry under the piano. She motions to me with her hands that there are bags to get. I carry them in without even realizing it. I am like a zombie. At one point I realize that it is nighttime but that is all. I spend the rest of that evening lying on my bed practically motionless. I picture Barry's face. From being so close to him in our living room, I recall that Barry actually has the faintest freckles. I never noticed them from a distance. This little imperfection makes him seem more desirable. That's when I admit to myself that I am in love with Barry Stillwater. I don't remember falling asleep. I have the most amazing dream. In my dream, there are thousands of earthworms. It feels like springtime. The black asphalt on the road glistens from wetness and sunlight. Everything is so green. I ask one of the earthworms something but I can't remember what I ask. The worm replies, "I'd rather be eaten than this." There is a patch of road where cars drive by, this one with fewer worms. They had been killed by the passing cars. I try to walk in the road. All I can remember is the rain. The nice quiet pellets that drop all around are mesmerizing. Suddenly I realize that I'd parked my car somewhere close, but now I can't find it. The dream moves me on. There's someone standing near me. I think it's Barry, but this guy has black hair. We're together and I set some papers on fire in a tin pan in an expanse of water (a lake?) by some boats. I can't remember if they are toy boats or real ones. He has a plump girl for a friend. We are at a dance. I sit next to him. She is on his lap. A really handsome guy asks her to dance. She says no but I encourage, or rather push her to go and dance with him. She reluctantly goes away. I am glad to be alone with him. He is telling me that we can be more open, or that he'll stop by after the dance. It is a Friday and I wonder if I'll ever be attracted to another but then I remind myself, Hold on to what you've got because you know that old lesson: you never know you have a good thing until you lose it.

The dream continues. I am snuggling up to his blue cotton pullover turtleneck while he smokes a cigarette. I pull a plastic chair closer but it is too low when I put it next to his. He doesn't care but I do. I go and get another one. When I return to the spot where we were sitting, he is gone. There is just his empty chair. I place my chair beside his now vacant chair. For some reason, I tell myself he went to look for his little brother.

So I sit and wait. The party has broken up and they are cleaning chairs in the other room. I thought that this one kid was giving me a chair but he walks past me. The chair is meant for another room. So, I slide myself over and sit in the chair of my lost love. I feel all alone. And then I wake up. I look at my clock; it is 3:30 in the morning. My lights are still on. I still have my clothes on. They are wet with sweat. I feel a panic come over me about what I'm feeling, and my dream. What had I done to Barry? Am I gay? I don't know. I can't get back to sleep at all; I just sit there with my portable CD player and ear phones. I turn out the lights and listen to some Lenny Kravitz. I can't explain what I'm thinking because I don't know myself. My portable CD player is sort of lame because once the CD is finished it keeps turning without any sound. I don't know how long I stay there. I fall asleep for what couldn't have been long when suddenly my alarm goes off. I groggily go downstairs to see that a plate of food was left out for me last night. Embarrassed, I quickly put the food in the fridge and the plate and utensils away. My mother is always asleep when I leave for school. At the bus stop there is no sign of Barry. Barry isn't in home room either. Barry doesn't show up until third period. We briefly glance at each other but don't say hi or anything. He gives me a grin hello. We avoid each other for the remainder of the day. As each minute passes my heart sinks a little further into despair. I want this day to end so I can go back to bed. But I can't, because tonight there is a game and I have to meet my father.

CHAPTER THREE

Basketball

quickly change and am about to join the others for the debriefing before tonight's game when Coach Murray calls me into his office. "Close the door son. I have to talk to you for a moment." I let a grin slip by me at the sound of Coach Murray calling me son. "Mark. A team is a team when every player plays his best and does what's best for the team." Here comes a sermon. I'm wondering where he is going with this, because I've greatly improved in my performance and I'm not lazy on the court, that's for sure. John Irving, our star player, usually doesn't hustle enough during warm-up drills, but coach doesn't push him because he's 6'4 and probably thinks that he needs to save his energy for the game. "Son, I can assure you that if someone is out or sick you'll be in there for the second string.""Whoa, what's this? I'm getting cut?" I interrupt. Coach Murray comes forward in his chair as if uneasy about my tone. "No, not cut Mark, it's just that I had to shuffle a few guys to add this new kid Barry. He was Markham District High's lead player. You'll play some games when we have someone absent, but since it's a two-tier team it just won't be that often."Rage overcomes me. In my mind, it is all Barry's fault. It feels as if someone punched me in the stomach. The coach goes on to say something about team spirit and being understanding but I just feel nauseous. So I sit at the bench through the entire game. I don't have the nerve to face my father, whom I'm sure is wondering what is going on.Since the divorce, I see my dad every other weekend, but he makes it a point to come to all my games when they are at home. Each district high school has two teams. The second string plays on court early. It is sort of a crowd teaser before the real games start. It is humiliating because our scores never count. Being benched means that I don't even get to wear a uniform. Dad's confusion shows on his face when I approach him fully clothed. I explain to him what happened, almost wanting to cry. Dad shrugs his shoulders and asks if I am all right with this decision. I lie and say yes. Why is he asking in that way? A sudden panic comes over me at the thought that my dad might mention his dissatisfaction to the coach. People are walking past us to take their seats for the game. He notices my discomfort on the subject and offers to take me out for a bite. I say sure. As we are leaving, I see Barry coming towards us. It looks like he is going to talk to me. Just then, my dad puts his arm on my shoulder. It is so strange that I turn to see what is touching my shoulder. When I look up Barry is gone. There are too many people around, and I'm not sure where he's gone. My dad pulls me towards him saying, "Don't worry, you are a great player." It feels nice to know that my dad is more concerned about how I feel than being disappointed. My dad has always carried a guilty conscience about the divorce and tries to overcompensate for his actions. I don't know exactly what lead to my parents separating, but I do remember the shouting. I must have tuned out the details. This evening turns out to be a real bonding experience because it is the first time my father tells me about himself, and it is very revealing. He tells me that when he was serving time in the army, his captain woke them up for a surprise search of their lockers. Dad, not being the morning person, complained, which was unheard of during that time. He tells me that it left a mark on his records that he carried throughout his service, denying him any promotions or possible service career. As I listen I forget about my own problems and take a realistic look at how much my father has sacrificed to be with me during my games. He had long ago started another family with his new wife and the games are the only time we are alone together. He seems not like a stranger but rather like a friend. My dad looks like a typical dad. He is balding, has a little more weight than is acceptable, but he has a cheerful face. We eat at Kelsey's, a well known restaurant chain in the city. Dad used to take me and mom here for my birthday. I have grown out of the place but it is the thought that counts. During dinner, dad and I go over every little humorous thing I did as a child, and reflect on our family outings. Those are the happier moments that he treasures, I guess. I start feeling nostalgic myself. It's fun. We really talk. When dad drops me off I'm really tired. I had so little sleep the night before. The house is dark. It is Friday so mom must be out showing houses. I don't bother turning on even one light. I climb upstairs and crawl into bed. In that moment all I can think of is Barry. He probably knew all along that this was going to happen to me. I hate him.

The next day Barry is waiting at the bus stop with Monica and a few other people. "Hey," he calls. Barry is smiling. I just stare and tell him that I was removed from the 2nd string basketball team. I ask if he knew anything about it. Noticing the seriousness in my face his smile changes to a stern look.

"Sort of," he replies.

"Sort of?" I yell while pushing him as hard as I can on the chest. He almost loses his balance. He looks at me like I'm crazy. "It's because of you," I shout while grabbing his shoulders. I feel flushed and on fire. He nervously looks around because by now everyone has crowded around us.

"Get your hands off me," he yells as he pushes me back. "You're just not as good as the others."

I feel my blood boil and I can hardly see. I lunge and grab at him again. "You liar," I scream.

"Get your fucking hands off me," he yells. "I don't like

being touched." He pushes me away and we are staring at each other, our chests heaving. "Since when?" I flatly ask. Without warning Barry slugs me so hard I fall to the ground. He is then on top of me, pounding me with his fists. "You faggot!" he is yelling. I am able to push him away but not before he gets in a few good punches. I'm struggling to keep my balance, and eventually manage to get in a few good shots, but I don't know where they land. Unfortunately, Barry appears to be a skilled brawler. I've never been in a serious fight before, ever. Just then the bus pulls up and the driver leaps out to separate us. It is then that I realize my nose is bleeding rather badly. "Break it up," the driver shouts. Our driver is Myrna and she's one tough lady. She practically tosses Barry on the bus and now the others are getting on. The driver looks at me and is reaching for the first aid kit. I feel like I am going to cry and don't want anyone to see so I shout, "That's all right," and I dash home as fast as I can. I enter through the back because I don't want them to see me fumble with the door, but I don't have a key for the back door. My head is pounding from the pain. There is blood everywhere. The driver eventually gets back on the bus and starts the engine. I see Barry's face in the window, searching for me. "Fuck you; fuck all of you," I shout. Then I start to cry. The bus is in the distance by the time I limp my way back to the front door and enter. My mom is in the kitchen with the radio on. "Honey!" she gasps in horror. "Who did this?" "It's nothing," I say as I try to get past her and go up the stairs to the bathroom. She follows me.

"Who did this?" When I don't answer she says she is calling the school. "No! Don't!" I shout in anger. "Honey, I have to!" she cries out from downstairs as she's thumbing through her phone book. I can already tell she has a cigarette in her mouth. I hate it when she calls me honey. It makes me feel like a child. Sometimes I feel so helpless I don't know what to do. She is dead set on calling the school. I sit on the edge of the bathtub and start to cry. "Mom!" She comes in and takes me in her arms and hugs me. My blood is staining her robe, but neither of us cares. She doesn't make the call. Alone again in the bathroom, I take a good look at the damage. My nose is all red but the bleeding has stopped. I wash the crusted blood from my face. I note that my left side is swollen and is going to bruise nicely. Mom drives me into school late. We don't say a word to each other. It is fourth period. It's one of the few classes I don't share with Barry. I am not concentrating at all. By this time the whole school has heard about the fight. I have this newfound popularity. I wonder exactly why it was that I had wanted his attention so badly. Could it be that my feelings are unnatural? His voice rings in my head. FAGGOT! I remember kissing him, but didn't he kiss me back? I then realize that for the past two weeks I've done nothing but think about him. Now I know our friendship has come to an end. I have never felt so alone in my life.

During the morning I manage to ignore Barry most of the time, but by lunch word has gotten out all over school about the fight. Todd Polino is the first to approach me. "Hey, slugger!" he croons, "I heard you got into a fight with Barry Stillwater. Is it true?" I really don't want to talk about it so I walk faster, but then Mark Macelli joins us.

"Way to go Mark. Is there going to be a rematch?" They chuckle. I laugh with them just to make it seem like I am cool with it. Then the bell rings and they dash away to their classes before I can say anything. The rest of the school day is one big sigh. It is raining when school ends. I know that usually after school Barry studies with Monica Llewellyn. They're neighbors. She's beautiful and is now even more popular with the cliques at school due to her relationship with Barry. For the rest of the week, Barry and I don't say much to each other. He is walking with Mark Macelli and the varsity basketball group. In fact, it's obvious we don't make any effort to see each other at all. My bruises are very evident and I feel so ugly all week. Barry doesn't even look at me. Barry eats elsewhere in the cafeteria with the varsity basketball crowd. Their clique grows because Monica's crowd has now joined them. It seems like they are one big happy family. However, there are moments when I'll glance over at Barry. He doesn't look back but he seems, among all these people, lonely. Each day during morning announcements, they talk about the upcoming basketball game for Friday. I cringe at the mention of anything to do with basketball. Sometimes, the thought of not playing on the team is so unbearable I want to cry, but I dare not in public. Barry doesn't sit near me on the bus and gets off at his regular stop. I don't go to the game on Friday. I leave a message for Dad not to come.

The next day, I wake up feeling really groggy. Thank god it is Saturday. I look at my clock. Noon! I make my way downstairs to the kitchen. Mom is in her bathrobe and slippers, cleaning under the sink. This is not normal because she usually is showing homes on the weekend.

"Morning sleepy head," Mom chirps in a bright and cheery voice. I almost never hear that voice. It is the sales voice she reserves for clients. "Listen, I have a doctor's appointment at 2:00 p.m., but I thought we'd go to the mall and get you some new clothes. You're looking a bit shabby these days."

"Ouch" I reply. We both laugh. I am happy to be getting some clothes. It just then dawns on me to get some Vans sneakers. I know Mom will not want to shell out the $175 for a pair of sneakers but somehow I have to convince her. The Oakville Mall is the closest mall to our house but our doctor's office is over by Fairview. Her doctor's visit is really brief. I could have waited in the car. I never really think of asking her why she has to go see a doctor, but then again we don't have that kind of relationship either. It is really crowded at the mall. Mom stops to look at every little thing, which annoys me. By now, we have hit almost every store except the one that I want to visit. This is bad because I don't want my mother to spend all her money before I get what I actually came here for. When we arrive at the shoe store with displays of Vans sneakers, I sort of put on a pouting face to get her attention.

She looks at me and asks, "Honey, do you see anything you like?" I take her to the Vans section. The sales girl approaches us. She is really short with black lipstick on her lips that makes her look like Wednesday from the Adam's Family. Contrary to her looks she is a little too cheerful for my liking. Each sneaker sample is on a rack covering an entire wall. The tags underneath clearly show the make and price of each sneaker.

"Looking for some Airwalks?" the sales girl asks.

"No, maybe something in a running sneaker," Mom replies, which is her way of saying these sneakers are too expensive. I look at the Airwalks and they are expensive but not as expensive as Vans. As she turns to head away from the Vans I interject, "Mom, I want these Vans sneakers in black suede." Mom looks at me like I just shot someone and checks out the sample I have in my hand. When mom sees the $175 tag on the shelf next to them she gets a real serious look on her face. She takes the sample sneaker from my hand and looks it over in detail. You can tell she thinks that they're not worth it. Before I allow her the chance to comment, I ask for size 11 in black. The sales girl disappears leaving me with a very disgruntled mother. Mom puts her store bags downs with all the items she purchased and waits for the sales girl to come back. Not even a fight or comment, which is so unlike my mother. Guilt rushes over me as I realize that I'm going to get away with this. I figure mom closed on those two houses and feels it is okay to treat me. Or at least I hope she's thinking this. The sales clerk comes back and drops three boxes of sneakers in front of us and rushes off to tend to other customers.

"In my day, they would put it on your foot and make sure it fits well," Mom grunts.

"It's the weekend and they're busy," I say. I open the first box. They are beige and not the style I want. I don't even wait. I close them and open the second box and see white ones but not the ones I asked for. I am beginning to get desperate thinking they don't have my style, but I am reassured when the last box I open has the black suede sneakers inside. I put them on and they feel awesome. "You are sure you want these?" Mom asks. "Yeah," I reply, "everyone at school has them." The sales clerk rings them up and hands over my sneakers in a bag the size of a blimp. As we enter the parking lot outside the mall, mom lights up a cigarette. Mom is quiet during the drive home and this makes me feel a little depressed. I hope she doesn't feel that she spent too much. I turn on the radio. Crowded House is playing.

When we get home, I run upstairs to put some of my new clothes away and to stare at my gorgeous new sneakers. I take them out and smell them. They don't have that suede smell I remember from when I was a kid and dad had that suede jacket. I dance around my room with them on. They feel fantastic on my feet and I am floating on air as I go downstairs to get a bite.

CHAPTER FOUR

Barry's House

Mom has fully changed clothes and is dressed to show homes. She is sitting on one of the stools by the counter, making phone calls. She reminds me between phone calls to make sure that I clean the den today. She adds that she wants me to be productive for the rest of the day and to not just sit in front of the television. I half listen to her say this while I am pouring a bowl of cereal. I sit and listen to her talk to her prospective clients. She is busy confirming people for an open house on Langley Avenue, out in Scarborough. I guess she does this to ensure heavy foot traffic instead of actually selling the place. She has a way of using this really phony real estate agent voice that annoys me. Mom always has these really frumpy suits on. They are tweed, like something one would imagine from the late '70s to early

'80s. I feel guilty for thinking this because I know we've been struggling since the divorce and she sacrifices so that I can have nice things. Mom's a chain smoker. She always has a cigarette in her hand. I feel sorry for her although we never speak about it. The divorce ruined her in a way. I never see her date anyone and she's always working. While I am deep in thought, I don't notice that she's talking to me. "Mark, will you do it?" Mom yells.

"What," I reply, equally as hostile, "the den?"

"No, could you give this packet to Mrs. Stillwater?" I freeze in silence. Does she know just exactly what she is asking of me? I feel trapped. I can't think of what to say. Reluctantly, as if defeated in battle, I say, "Alright." I close my eyes, wishing I had stayed more attentive and been able to think of a good argument. Something like, "They are around the corner so couldn't you just drop it off yourself?" I watch her as she finishes her last call, grabs her purse and snuffs out her cigarette in the ashtray on the table. She then grabs her coat off the couch, puts it on, and looks at herself in the mirror in the foyer. She seems displeased with her reflection. She runs her hands through her hair and when she convinces herself she's made some improvements, she walks out the door. I hear her footsteps and the car door open and shut. Taggs comes into the kitchen and puts his paws on my lap. Then there is silence. She is probably looking for a cigarette in her bag. After a minute or so, I hear her start the car, put it into gear and drive off down the road. She is gone and the whole house is silent again. I look down at Taggs and realize what I have to do. I turn on the radio and old '80s tunes are playing. I like the song but can't remember who sings it. I 'm in my room ripping off the annoying plastic anchors that hold price tags to clothing. I'm trying on one outfit after the other. I don't have a full-length mirror in my room and have to run down to the foyer to check myself out. After four or five flights up and down the stairs I'm beginning to feel tired. I finally decide on the green pullover shirt mom and I just bought at the Gap, and add a dirty t-shirt and jeans. I don't remember if Barry was wearing black or white socks with his Vans but I decide on my white ones. I take one last look at myself in the mirror. I comb my hair over and over again and then decide to run back up to the bathroom out of frustration, to wet my hair and comb it again. I finally decide it's no use and grab my jacket and run outside making sure not to let Taggs out. It's chilly and already dark out. It must be around 7 p.m. I'm at the end of our driveway when I remember that I left Mrs. Stillwater's packet on our kitchen counter. I curse myself under my breath and run back inside. Once outside again, I am walking at a fast, nervous pace. I'm excited at having a reason for going to Barry's house. I'm walking down the street and there are about three houses and then a field where there should be a house at the corner of Ashford and Hemmington. It is really chilly out. I wonder why there isn't a house there, or on the lot next to it. The lot next to it is clearly on Hemmington. It must be older because they have mature trees situated everywhere. The houses on Ashford are noticeably older and smaller. Our house, like all the others on Ashford, is painted various somber colors, whereas the homes on Hemmington are very grand with long driveways, nice landscaping, lampposts, and stained wood instead of paint. I am not exactly sure which house is the Stillwaters'. I look at the package and lift it closer to see the address mom wrote. I notice my hand is shaking from the excitement. I feel really flushed and my heart is pounding. 83 Hemmington Drive. I look up and have to practically trespass on every front lawn to read the numbers on the houses. By the time I pass the house marked 76 I am sure that the house ahead will be Barry's. It fits with that all-too-perfect family image, sitting atop a little hill. The driveway slopes on the right so the garage doesn't face the street, but rather the side. There is a shiny Jag parked in the driveway. It is too dark to make out what color. I know it's a Jaguar because the pouncing, big cat ornament is so visible on the hood. The house is dark but the lights from inside indicate that there is someone home. I wonder which window is Barry's room. As I turn and walk up the sloping driveway a light from over the garage goes on. It blinds me and I think of just dropping the mail in the mailbox at the foot of the driveway. My heart is pounding like it's going to explode. I walk along the path that leads to the double front doors with stained glass side windows. It looks really nice. The grounds are obviously landscaped. The stained glass seems like the perfect touch of detail, like something that would be highlighted in that old show with Robin Leach, Lifestyles of the Rich and Famous. I ring the doorbell and hear it echo throughout the house. I hear nothing for a minute except my heart pounding, my breathing heavy. Then I see a small silhouette through the stained glass approach the door. A porch light goes on, just as bright as the garage one that blinded me earlier. The door opens and I feel the heat of the house escape. A pretty young girl peers out from the large door but says nothing. She must have been seven or eight. She doesn't really look like Barry but I can see they have the same eyes. "Hi, I'm Mark Thomas." My voice cracks right when I say Thomas. I just want to crawl under a rock and die. Why did I say my last name? The door closes but then swings ajar just a little. "Mom!" I hear her scream as she goes running off into the back of a long hallway that leads to what looks like the kitchen. I don't get a chance to inform her that I have a package or anything. Seizing the opportunity, I slip into the house. This is so unlike me but I figure this is my one chance to get a look into the world of Barry Stillwater. I quietly wait there in the dark foyer, but no one approaches me. I don't see anything except a staircase leading up to my right. I see a little light from the top of the stairs but no sounds. To my left is the living room. It is dark but I can make out furniture from what little street light illuminates the room. I hear a kitchen fan over a stove coming from directly ahead. Getting antsy, I walk towards the light. I don't even take off my new Vans. As I enter, I know it's the kitchen. The kitchen table is a large oak table with eight high-backed chairs standing to the right of me. Six places have been set. To my embarrassment, I see that they haven't eaten yet. The regular kitchen counters and appliances are on the left side of the room. What is strange about the layout is that there is a fireplace behind the kitchen table. It is waist high and obviously gas, but on its other side is another room. There are stairs, maybe four or five of them that lead to a room along the back wall. Through the double-sided gas fireplace I can see carpeting and the little girl that let me in is lying down in front of the TV. I can faintly hear an old Star Trek: The Next Generation episode. Pots with food on them are on the stove. I feel that I have walked into a Crisco commercial because I can smell delicious fried chicken, and the kitchen looks so clean and new. I hear footsteps from behind me and I quickly swing around just in time to see a lady enter the kitchen. I am so startled that I drop the package on the floor. It is obvious that she didn't hear the young girl call because she is annoyed that I'm here. I'm sure it's Barry's mom because she has the same piercing eyes as Barry. What is more intriguing is that she is stunningly beautiful. Her hair is a shiny black like the young girl's. It is long but pulled back behind her ears. She is wearing dangling silver earrings. She is thin but not too thin. She has on a powder blue dress and navy heels. I would have thought her to be some sort of royalty. I think she looks expensive, but I'm certain she's the most beautiful mother I've ever seen, if she is Barry's mother. To save any further embarrassment, or to break my staring, I introduce myself as Mark Thomas, Leila Thomas's—the realtor's— son. This doesn't change her mood one bit. I hand over the package, mumbling something about my mom asking me to give this to her. She mutters a polite hello and takes the package, placing it on the counter before going to check on the food cooking on the stove. Just then, I hear more rumbling from the stairs; the whole house is coming to life, and two boys, one being Barry and another taller one, barrel into the kitchen. Barry isn't paying attention because he is busy pulling a shirt over his head. I catch just enough of his torso to see that fine line of belly hair.

When he sees me he stops with a skid and his mouth drops open. The taller guy immediately sits down at the farthest corner of the kitchen table. Barry looks nervously toward his brother and then back to me. I am hoping to be beamed up into an old episode of Star Trek, but I know this isn't going to happen. Not knowing what to do, I call, "Hey Barry," in the most superficial voice I can muster. I add an even worse smile, imagining how my mom does it during her house viewings. The strangest thing is that he smiles even more and says hi back.

Just then, Barry's mother touches my shoulder with an oven mitt to get by me to put something on the table. I practically jump into Barry's arms to get out of her way. The brother laughs like it is the funniest thing. I pull away from Barry. I know for sure my face is red enough to stop cars in the street. Barry is pissed off and grabs some papers off the counter and throws them at him. "Shut up!" Barry yells. Barry's mom throws him a stern expression of warning. As I'm explaining to Barry about my delivery, the front door opens and a man approaches from behind Barry. He is really tall and has blondish grey hair. He still has his jacket on and is carrying a brown paper bag in his arms. The man looks serious but brightens up when he catches sight of me.

"Who's this?" he asks. Barry swings around and tells him that I'm a friend from school.

"It's the realtor's son," the woman adds. The man introduces himself as Barry's father and extends his hand. I shake it. My hand seems so small in comparison, but his gentleness puts me at ease.

"Are you staying for supper?" he asks, but he isn't looking at me, but rather at Barry's mom. I denote a slight accent in his voice but can't make it out. Barry's mom seems indifferent to the suggestion but offers me a seat. I look at Barry who is smiling at me in the strangest way.

"No, I ate already, but thank you," I reply. Barry's smile turns to a frown. I feel confused by this behaviour. "Well, maybe some other time then," Mr. Stillwater adds as he goes back down the foyer and up the stairs. There is a long pause. I feel like everyone is staring at me, and I'm nervous, so I blurt out, "I guess I should go now." I start heading towards the front door. Barry follows me. I open the door and am already outside when Barry yells, "Wait!" almost as though in frustration. I turn around and he is leaning outside the door with one hand on the frame. Barry comes outside and closes the door. It's so cold out I can see the clouds of his breath. There's a long pause. He's staring at the ground. "Are you okay?" he asks, looking up nervously. I'm trying to look anywhere but at him. I'm feeling anxious. I don't answer, just look around, shifting my weight from one foot to the other, like he's occupying my time. "Wait here" he says, and he runs into the house. I hear him bolt up the stairs. A light comes on in the far right corner of the upstairs. Question answered . . . his room. He returns with a wrapped package in his hands. He gives it to me. "I guess this doesn't make up for what I did but I wanted to say I'm sorry." He holds it out. I don't take it but rather I stare in amazement. My heart is beating and I lose my cool and break out into the dorkiest smile ever seen. "Well, don't let my arm fall off," he says. I take it. I sort of laugh and feel myself blushing.

"Thanks," I say, holding it in my hands, not knowing what to do. "Well, open it," he says with an excited look on his face. I hesitate. I want to take it home and just stare at the package all night. "I want to open it at home," I say. "Why don't you eat at my house?" He pauses, which annoys me and my smile is lost. Seeing this he gets nervous and quickly says yes to appease me. "Hold on." He runs inside. I peer through the stained- glass. His family by now has started to eat. I see him go in and ask. I hear a muffled, "No," but Barry raises his voice and starts back towards me, grabbing his coat that's hanging on a hook on the wall in the foyer. His mom is starring at us through the window in annoyance. I guess she thinks I'm trouble or something. I'm thinking to myself that this is a dumb idea because I already ate and I don't cook well. I don't even know what is in the house to eat. Barry shuts the door behind him and says, "Let's go." He grabs the wrapped package from my hands, flashes it in front of my face and goes racing down the street towards my house. He's really fast because I'm running with all my might trying to catch up to him. He slows down just to tease me. We get to my door totally out of breath. We're leaning against my outside door side-by-side. I'm trying to catch my breath. I can hear Taggs going wild on the other side. I have to admit all this excitement is overwhelming. I get the key and open the door. Taggs is jumping all over us. "Hey there, buddy," Barry says, and he leans down to play with the dog. The kitchen light is on. Mom or I must have forgotten to turn it off. I turn on the radio and blast it real loud. Barry and Taggs trail along into the kitchen. I open the fridge and throw Barry a can of Coke. I thought that would be cool to do. "Hey, it'll fizz now!" Barry protests while laughing. "Oh yeah, sorry," I say in embarrassment. I turn to look in the fridge. Barry comes and stands beside me very close and looks in too. His closeness makes me feel funny. I don't want to move away. I see some shrimp and rice. I ask him if he likes Chinese. While eyeing the shrimp on the lower shelf, he asks if I have any curry. He says he likes spicy food. I say yes, but I admit that I don't know how to make it. Barry takes over and grabs the shrimp and I get my mom's wok. We're like two chefs singing in the kitchen. Barry is cutting the veggies and I am heating the oil and adding the shrimp. We dance to the music playing in the background. Barry takes charge when it comes time to add the seasoning while I stir our concoction. Barry leans over the wok to smell it and, stupid me, without warning I kiss his cheek. He looks at me in surprise. I quickly turn away. "I think we have some almonds to add. Do you like them?" I go to the fridge and grab a Coke to hide my embarrassment. When I turn around Barry is stirring the shrimp and veggies. He isn't looking at me as I had thought. I pull out some silverware and two plates. Mom and I had some cooked rice the other night, so I microwave the leftovers and scoop a pile on each of the plates. Barry soon follows, placing equal portions of the shrimp stir fry over the rice. We sit across from each other at the table. Every now and again, Barry tosses a veggie or shrimp at Taggs. Taggs catches them flawlessly. "Cut it out," I tease, "We don't have enough shrimp for all three of us." Barry then takes some of his shrimp and puts it on my plate. I feel ashamed for complaining. "Thanks," I say. Barry beams with a grin as if to say, "Don't mention it." He has a way of acting like he is Mr. Cool. Eating with him is awkward. We don't say much. Every now and then I catch him looking my way. His cell phone rings but he doesn't answer it; he just looks at it and pushes a button to silence it. "Are you going to the dance," he asks me while putting his phone back into his pocket. I haven't given it much thought. I nod to avoid the question about whom I would be bringing. We finish eating. I don't offer dessert, nor does he ask. I remember that Mom rented some videos which I had yet to return. There is probably one incredibly huge late fee sitting on our account. We dump the dishes in the sink and Barry follows me down to the den. I'm embarrassed by our 80's-style furniture, remembering that Barry's family's furniture looks new and in style, at least from what I saw of it. Also, to add insult to injury, I hadn't cleaned up earlier, so it is still quite messy. I had hoped one of the films would be to his liking, but he is indifferent when I show him the selection. I chose a random movie which I will not remember later. Our couch in the den is small and I make it a point to let Barry sit down first. I don't want to do something stupid like that kiss again. I turn the lights out and sit on the floor against the couch. Taggs comes over and lies down on my lap. About twenty minutes into the movie, I look behind me and Barry is sound asleep. He looks so peaceful. He shifts on the couch, and suddenly his hand is sticking out beside me. I want to kiss him again so badly, but restrain myself. Instead, I slowly put my hand into his. He doesn't flinch or move at all. It doesn't wake him. My palms are sweaty. His are warm and dry. They smell of curry and onion. I turn to watch the rest of the movie. I am in an awkward position to be holding his hand while facing the TV, but I don't care. Towards the end of the film Barry shifts position again, and this causes my hand to fall off. But his hand is now by my face and I am satisfied. It is so close I can feel his warmth. From time to time, I brush my cheek up to his hand. I feel so content. Taggs at one point moves from my lap and jumps up on the couch and curls up by Barry's feet. Taggs isn't supposed to be on the couch but it is such a Hallmark moment that I let him stay. While I'm watching the film, Barry's voice says softly, "How long have I been sleeping?"

I turned and lie, "I don't know."

Barry's cell phone rings again but he ignores it. "You haven't opened your gift." Our faces are so close I can smell the curry on his breath. I go to get the wrapped gift that is sitting on the kitchen counter. I stumble on the first stair but quickly regain my balance. It is really dark in the den with the only illumination coming from the TV. When I return Barry is sitting up. I don't turn on the light. I run my hands over the wrappings. I really don't want to open it, but I don't want to seem rude, so I begin to tear at the paper. It is a dark blue pullover. It is really nice. "I hope it fits," he says. I hold it up and thank him. I get up and go to the foyer mirror. Barry follows. I flinch because he turns on the foyer light and suddenly I 'm in the mirror. My heart is thumping loudly. Everything seems to be in brilliant colors. Barry stands just behind me. I'm holding the shirt up and it fits perfectly. We stare at each other through the mirror. At one point, he's staring at the scar on my face from our fight. "I really am sorry," he says. I almost ask what about, but then I remember and stop myself. I just smile. I can tell how sorry he is. I don't know how long we are standing there. I feel the pressure of a hard-on in my pants, but thankfully my new shirt keeps it out of view. The white noise from the TV breaks our stare. "Well, I should go," he says. He heads towards the door and I lean in to pull the door open for him and that's when he kisses me. Not like that silly kiss I gave him earlier in the kitchen, but rather a soft, long kiss on the lips. It is like the ones you see in the movies. He pulls back. This whole situation confuses me but I don't want it to go away. He looks down and then looks away and then he's gone. I want to watch him fade into the distance, but the glass on the outer door fogged up too fast; so I close the door and lean against it for awhile. "I want to know what you're thinking, Barry," I say to myself. The house seems empty now. I go upstairs and lay in bed, re-enacting in my mind the kiss over and over again. I wouldn't change this day for the world.

CHAPTER FIVE

The Game

We have another home game the next day, and it's the last game before our school dance. The game begins. Barry is playing and he is absolutely focused and determined to win. I break my long avoidance of game attendance, thinking this might be good for me. Ten minutes into the game I know this is going to be a difficult match for the team, and I feel sick to my stomach with nerves. I can tell that the opposing team has identified Barry as our key player and they are blocking passes to him left and right. I can see that Barry is giving one hundred and ten percent playing this game, but we are still down by six points. Our opponents have surpassed our expectations; they are a strong team, much more potent than any of the teams we've challenged before. I can tell that they are just as determined as our team to win this game. The crowd is hungry for battle. The noise levels are deafening and it's hard to concentrate. It's not a surprise that this team made it to the finals last year because they most definitely carry strong players. Even so, only one team is going home with the win and I hope it's us. I see Monica there with her gaggle of girls. She has her eye on Barry the entire game. She is a cheerleader, so she shouts out his name and gets the rest of the girls to follow suit. It really angers me that I can't shout out Barry's name without calling unwanted attention to myself. I ponder this for a moment and wonder if I am being too paranoid. I hear other guys shout out his name from the bleachers behind me.One night while we were walking Taggs Barry told me that he has been playing basketball ever since he was six years old, with his brother and his father. I know there have been quite a few scouts from universities looking at him.The game lasts into overtime. It is tied 108 to 108. I am so hoarse from screaming. The opposing team is pretty good at keeping Barry blocked for most of the game but they get lazy because our team switched to a new strategy that doesn't involve Barry as much. With only five seconds left on the clock our team is down by one point. These five seconds will determine who wins the game. Just then, Barry breaks away from the guards, catches a ball, runs it up the court, and with less than a second to spare, he slam dunks it in, winning the game. The hysterical crowd spills out into the court and hoists Barry into the air. It happens so suddenly even Barry is shocked. I happily watch the celebrations for a little while, but then I slip out to go home. It is late and I am tired but I have to take Taggs out for his walk.

Taggs and I travel over our normal loop through the woods and return to go back home. When we come out, Barry is waiting for us. Taggs runs to jump up on him and I follow. "I saw you at the game; you should have waited for me to shower and we could have walked home together." I can tell he is a little pissed.

I am glad that he wants me to be with him and I really have no answer for him except, "Sorry." "I skipped my shower, so I must stink. I tried to catch up with you, but I guess I just missed you." My mind races with thoughts of Barry wanting to chase after me. It is overwhelming. I try to change the subject by making a joke about him stinking. He makes a fake laugh, drops his duffel bag and looks at Taggs. "Should we get him boy! Let's get him." And he rushes to tackle me to the ground. He lifts my coat and shirt in the area around my stomach and starts to tickle me. I laugh uncontrollably and Taggs is barking and licking my face. It's fun. We're both exhausted and out of breath. It is cold. My shirt and coat are still pulled up and Barry is resting his head on my stomach. Just then he gets up, rifles through his duffel bag and pulls out a pen. I pull my shirt and coat back down because I am freezing. I stare at Barry. Barry pushes me back down and pulls my coat and shirt back up and writes something just above my belly button. I look down and it is a phone number. I smile. I'm guessing it's his cell phone.

He is staring back with Taggs in his arms, licking his face. "I'd better go," he says. "I really need to shower." He gets up, picks up his duffel bag and walks away. I grab Taggs so he won't trail after him. I watch him fade into the night.

CHAPTER SIX

School Dance

School dances are lame. It's Monday and now everyone is talking about it. The dances are usually on a Friday. The school social committee, which is comprised of half the cheerleading squad and half of the band, stays after school to prepare and decorate the whole school. They often decide on really weird themes for school dances. The last one I can remember was The Love Boat after the old TV series. This time it's a Cupid theme, even though Valentine's Day was months ago. Although most people go stag, the basketball team, football, and other high school sports-team members usually have dates.

The fact that Barry asks me about the dance makes me want to go. He doesn't ask me to the dance, but rather he inquires. I am not much of a social person to begin with, and the thought of going to one of these events scares me to death. But something makes me go. Barry eats lunch with me almost every single day. His presence at my table attracts many unwelcome visitors. Mainly it's Todd, Judy Aronson (Todd's girlfriend), Monica Llewellyn and their friends. However, it doesn't bother me now, nor does it bother me that they are engrossed in conversations that I rarely take part in. It feels like I am the big secret in Barry's life and no one knows but me. This somehow makes me feel superior to all of them. I actually feel cool. "What do you think, Mark?" I hear a female voice say. It is Monica. "Oh, I'm sorry. What did you say?" I reply. I blush when I realize that all eyes at the table are on me now. "I think you should ask Krista Woods to the dance." Monica repeats. "You think?!" I answer back, which brings laughter from all around, including Barry. Barry joining in with them in the laughter angers me. Krista and I have known each other since the second grade. If it weren't for her growing up I would have never been invited to any of the birthday parties in the neighborhood. Monica, not being amused, turns to Judy and complains about boys not being mature enough to ask someone out. Judy agrees while clinging to Todd, and is clearly not interested in the topic. She prefers gazing at Todd while chewing loudly on her bubble gum.I am somehow gaining new status at school due to my association with Barry, our big fight, and then our friendship. He is becoming quite the noticeable athlete for the basketball team. Since he's joined we've been undefeated. The school paper did an "upfront and personal" article on Barry, as they do from time to time on other key players and student leaders. I see the picture of him in his basketball uniform on the front page, with the title: Barry, the Man, the Legend. Boy, does he ever get teased about that one. I usually don't read the paper right away. Instead I save it until I am alone in my room so I can read it comfortably. It asks him a series of questions about his family, what he plans to do, etc. I feel the headline should have read: Barry, Man of Mystery, because of his vague, one-word answers. All I get out of it is that he has an older brother and a younger sister. They want a bigger house and he doesn't miss his last school. However, there is one question that does stick in my mind. The question is: Any love interests, and if so, is this person at school? Barry's answer: Yes, yes. I laugh when I read it but there is a big doubt in my head and a real touch of insecurity in his answer.

Friday comes and goes like a flash of lightning. Everyone is excited about the school dance. I hear shouts of people passing by, saying, "See you there." I don't realize at first that most of these comments are for me. I will have to work on my new public image. By the time I get home, I am really excited, but time is passing by at a much slower pace. The house is empty. I play with Taggs for a few minutes after our walk. I cook myself a lame meal of microwave soup and begin getting ready for the dance. Is it the thought of seeing Barry? I decide it will be cool to wear the blue pullover that Barry gave me. I haven't actually worn it yet. I take it out of the closet and stare at it. It still has all the tags on it. I shower and shave, although I don't really need to shave, and get dressed. I can't tell if the shirt makes me look as attractive as I feel, or is it just because Barry gave it to me. I think about calling Barry but I don't.

This time I walk to school. As I approach I hear the loud noises and cars pulling up and dropping off people. The school looks so different at night. It's really cold out. I hurry my pace to get out of the cold. When I get there, I feel my heart pounding. I am in the lineup for raffle tickets, scouting the room for Barry when I hear a voice calling out to me. "Mark, I don't think I've ever seen you out." I look down and it is Krista Wood.

"Hey Krista, long time no see," I say, smiling one of mom's fake smiles. I feel I should smile more with my newfound popularity. Krista is very short but really nice. I can see that she dressed up for the dance. She has her hair curled and is wearing lots of make-up. Her dress is red velvet. I think it makes her hips look too wide, but women's hips are always wide. We keep together even after we get our tickets. The gym has been transformed for the dance. It is dark except for the flashing lights. I can tell it was done by one of those DJ companies that set up and run school dances. Still, the layout is impressive. The volunteers really did a good job. Krista and I walk around, catching up on old times. I try to act interested but all the while I am really straining to find where Barry is in the crowd.

"Monica said we should have all come together, but you didn't want to?" I don't remember ever saying that and I'm wondering what's up. Krista and I get some sodas and stroll around some more. We said hi to a couple of people and make small talk. It is an hour into the dance when people start dancing. Although I don't usually dance, Krista is real pushy on the subject so I do. We dance a little but I am still searching for him. Krista remarks that she likes my sweater. It is getting pretty hot in the pullover but I dare not take it off; I feel as though it is sacred.

I'm just about to motion us to exit the dance floor when Judy and Todd dance alongside us. Krista and Judy are whispering in each other's ears, which I think is rude and annoying. Todd is just bouncing to the music. He has to be the lamest dancer I have ever seen. I chuckle to myself. "Have you seen Barry?" I ask Todd. "Yeah, he's over there with Monica," he says, pointing to a dark corner where the chairs are. I make a mental note to meander over there after dancing with Krista. It seems like this song is going to go on forever. Todd mentions that Billy Compton is getting expelled, saying that there is a chance that I'll get back on the team. I take it as an insult, but I know he is trying to make small talk and he is sincere in what he's saying. Another song comes on and I start gesturing to Krista that I'm leaving, but she begs for just one more dance. I oblige her. I don't really want to dance again. I am overheating from wearing the "sacred" pullover and I really want to find Barry. The song is one I like and I compliment Krista on her choice. She seems to take it like I told her she is beautiful or something. When it ends, I say that I'll be back and quickly leave, purposely not giving Krista a chance to object or follow. The area which Todd pointed out is quite dark. There are several figures sitting about and I think it will be impossible to make them out. As my eyes become accustomed to the dark, I realize that the two people right in front of me are Monica and Barry, making out passionately. They don't see me. All emotions and feelings drain away from me. I feel a pain in my chest. As I back away, I bump noisily into some chairs. I quickly turn and run across the gym floor. I hurry out into the hallway towards the door, and then I hear footsteps running behind me. I know its Barry. I start running as fast as I can. Tears are running down my face. By now we are out on the field in front of the school. "Wait," I hear him call. I feel him gaining on me. By the time I reach the hill that leads to the road Barry has caught up to me. His hand grabs at my pants as he tries to pull me back. I stop running and swing around like I'm ready to fight. I make two fists, poised like a boxer. In hindsight, I must have looked silly. I lunge at Barry but he pushes me aside. Tears are streaming down my face, I must look stupid but I don't care. I go at him again but he grabs me and is about to strike me with a fist when he realizes what he is about to do. "No, I'm not going to fight you Mark!" he yells. "Like hell you won't!" I scream in all my rage. I feel the tears flowing everywhere. I am crazed, mad. He manages to wrestle me to the ground without fighting me. I keep screaming, "I hate you. I fucking hate you!" By now I am really bawling. Barry has me pinned down with his knees on my shoulders and his hands hold my fists above my head. I see that my words have wounded him. He doesn't say anything, he just lets me cry. Luckily, we aren't within earshot of anyone at the bottom of the hill where no one can see us. We are breathing heavily. I start to calm down. I am still crying, though I don't care. I don't know what to say except that I am mad. Mad at what? It is then that I realize that I am truly in love with Barry Stillwater. It is me that wants to be making out with him passionately in that corner of the gym. It is in this moment that I realize that I am gay. No words come to me that can express these feelings to Barry. So I cry some more to myself. "I know you saw me with Monica, Mark," he whispers. "I couldn't stop her, or do anything." He rolls off me and sits there staring into space. "When she was touching me, I had to think of you, Mark." Whoa, I shout in my head. I turn onto my side. I can't believe what I'm hearing. Just then he starts crying and it is more like a whimper than an all-out cry. "Why did you try to start a fight with me? I don't want to hit you – that's the last thing I want to do, Mark!" My head starts spinning. I want to feel joyous but instead I feel stupid, ashamed, and very confused. "Dude, we've got to change," I say, but it comes out all wrong. He looks at me in an odd sort of way. "I mean we have to get this out in the open because," I clarify. My heart starts pounding, "I have feelings for you." Barry wipes his eyes. They are red. He looks so vulnerable.

He starts to shiver because it is cold outside here on the damp grass. He gets up and I note the details of his muscular legs outlined against his pants as he rights himself. He pauses for a moment.

"Let's go talk," he says, looking straight ahead instead of at me. I turn away and head for the school but he doesn't move.

"Don't you want to get your jacket?" He just shakes his head and heads towards our neighborhood. Somehow, I feel he is angry. We walk for a long time. Our heavy breathing from our running on the field has tired us out. I can't stand the silence anymore. "Are you mad at me?" I ask after a long moment of silence.

"No," he replies, looking at me, "and stop being so down on yourself, Mark. It's not you. It's me. I'm mad at myself for not talking earlier." He says this in an annoyed way. We continue walking a bit longer in silence. Like an idiot, I have to go and open my big mouth. "Well, it takes two to talk so I should have said something also." This comment makes Barry burst out with laughter. I laugh too, given the inane comment I have just made. It actually breaks the ice. Barry starts talking more about himself and his life. I convince myself that I should remain absolutely silent from this point on and just listen to him. He tells me that he takes after his mom. They both lack good communication skills. He keeps trying to be "in my space" to facilitate more interaction between us, hoping his feelings will come out or that he'll say something. He even admits that he had started waiting at my bus stop in order to see more of me. The mere thought that Barry thinks of me so much is overwhelming. It gives me a splitting headache, but a happy one; I can hardly believe it. This was when Monica started following him there and hanging out there too. Barry says he knows he has feelings for both guys and girls. This statement hurts but I understand what he means. By now, we have passed my house. I am growing concerned about the cold air and Barry without a jacket, but he keeps walking and talking. He says he honestly feels bad about my leaving the team and that he personally spoke to the coach to try and change his mind, but it didn't work. He really feels bad about calling me a faggot and everything, and he continues to ramble on and on. I am just pleasantly surprised. I don't think he's spoken like this ever. I catch bits and pieces of what he is saying but am too overwhelmed to get the gist of it.We have reached his house. It is visibly empty. I feel uncomfortable being there but he pulls out his cell phone and keys from his pocket and we enter through a side door. He clicks on a light and keeps walking. The hallway smells of cinnamon and cloves; I'm not sure if those are the correct spices, but the smell is pleasant. We walk up the stairs and into the kitchen. He grabs a paper towel, runs it under the tap and gives it to me. "You might want to fix yourself up." I look for the bathroom. Barry notices what I am looking for and points to the hall towards the foyer. I go in there and see that I'm pretty messed up. There's grass and dirt stuck to my face, mixed in with the sweat and tear streams that have dried. My hair is all over the place with dirt and crap in it! I hurriedly try to tidy myself. When I come out Barry is standing in front of the fridge with the door open, just staring. "Don't throw me a Coke," I joke, trying to break the ice; but he doesn't hear me and just looks up. Too bad Taggs isn't here to put us at ease. The house is warm and I really would like to have a look around. I hint that I want to look around, which snaps him out of his weird mood. He then gives me the grand tour. First we go into the living room, located at the front of the house. It is really nice but you can tell that it is only for show because Barry doesn't even walk in there. It has white carpeting. The furniture is nice and expensive-looking with dark wood finishing. It looks like everything was laid out for a furniture catalogue shoot: the kind with too much furniture, with every corner occupied, candles everywhere, and magazines and porcelain fruit in a bowl on the coffee table. Then he goes up the stairs and I see his room, his sister's room, his brother's room and his parents' room. The bedrooms are smaller than I expected. Even the master bedroom is small. However, they are still bigger than the rooms in our house. I notice that the Stillwaters don't have a guest room, whereas we do. Then again, there are five people in their family, as opposed to our two. When the tour is over we return, as I had hoped, to Barry's bedroom. Barry turns on the stereo and hops onto the bed. I don't know whether to sit on the bed or the chair. I try to play it cool and walk around the room a bit, looking at things in detail. I am sort of studying his room, committing it to memory. He really has a lot of sports stuff on the walls: ribbons, medals and trophies. He seems to have always been on varsity leagues. Books are scattered all over his desk. I must have taken awhile. "Are you going to search the drawers too?" he chuckles. I turn to him and comically say, "Yes!" and continue my inspection with a smile. He offers me something to drink and leaves to go get it. I want him to stay but am also grateful because it gives me time to actually snoop further into his belongings. Weird as it may sound, I open his closet. There is a cord for the light and I yank on it. There is plenty in there. His clothes seem cramped but orderly. The tidiness surprises me. Shoes and sneakers are on the floor. I get nervous and quickly close the doors again. I can hear him in the kitchen and then his footsteps walking up the stairs. When he reappears, I am nonchalantly standing by the window. "All we have is Coke," he informs me as he hands over the glass. It has gone flat but I don't mind. He gets back on the bed and motions for me to come and lay down next to him. His bed is small but we manage to squeeze on. Staring up at his ceiling, I notice it is covered with glow-in-the-dark stars. They seem kind of childish but I don't say anything. Barry explains that he used to collect them. He got his first set from a cereal box when he was seven or eight years old. He'd make his mom buy boxes and boxes of cereal even though he got tired of the cereal after the first box. I laugh at his story of how he'd get up early and dump the cereal in the garbage can just to get another box with the stars inside. After the promotion was over from the cereal company, Barry then found a store that carried similar stars. He points out each constellation, and tells me how he learned the names of each cluster. Each night when he went to sleep he'd recount them, making a sort of game of it, naming each star as if counting sheep until he got tired. He tells me they were the first things he put up in his room when he moved here. We are quiet for awhile and then Barry rises up onto his elbow and gazes down at me. I smile back and am about to saying something like, "How about OUR TALK?" but he leans over and starts kissing me before I have a chance to speak. Our kissing becomes pretty serious. I feel him slide his hand around my waist as he moves on top of me. He feels heavy and good and I am getting an erection. He gets up and closes the door and turns the lights off, which freaks me out a little, but then he turns on the lamp that stands by his desk. He comes back and plops right on top of me, knocking the wind out of me. We both laugh. He doesn't give me enough time to comment as he starts to kiss me again. As we are making out, I run my hands nervously along his sides. He seems really solid, firm. I guess I must feel the same way to him. I am really curious to feel whether he has a hard-on or not because I am sure he can feel mine. We stop briefly to take our shirts off. I again see that thin line of sexy hair on his lower torso and realize I hadn't seen it for a long time. I feel embarrassed by my practically hairless body and start hoping he'll turn all the lights out. But he doesn't. He resumes kissing and touching me all over. He is again on top of me and

I am really getting caught up in the moment. He slowly moves his hand between us to my pants. He runs his fingers along the rim of my pants and my skin. It feels good. He then slowly moves his hand deeper inside. I almost want to stop him, but a greater part of me wants to do the same thing to him. However, it's difficult to maneuver from my position. Barry opens my pants button and slides down the fly. He presses his hand along my pelvis as he loosens my restricting pants. I can go further but then it won't be special to me anymore. I can say this: Barry smells of warm milk and cologne. What kind of cologne I don't know. We squeeze and rub and eventually jerk each other off. It is rather sweaty and urgent and messy and exciting all at the same time. Afterwards, we get cleaned up. Barry uses tissues to wipe away the sticky mess, whereas back at home if I was by myself I'd use a towel. He then turns the lights out and returns to bed. He and I are on our sides facing each other. In my head I hear this favorite old school song of Monica's playing, called Angel of Mine, as I drift off to sleep. Occasionally, I hear the muffled sound of Barry's cell phone, which he doesn't answer, and this disrupts my sleep, but I quickly drift off again. Barry is a heavy sleeper. We never do get around to speaking about the incident at the dance. Throughout the night, I listen to him breathing peacefully beside me. We both squirm and shift around often because the bed is too small and really quite uncomfortable.

CHAPTER SEVEN

Breakfast

wake up to strange noises coming from the hallway. My shoulders are cold and I am butt naked. I panic. It is daylight out. However, I am in the bed all by myself. I am under the covers but don't remember how I got there. I am foggy and confused for a moment as to where I am, but only for a split second because I quickly remember where I am, and the realization snaps me awake. I look around to find Barry asleep on the floor, wrapped up in a comforter and two pillows. "Barry, get up, your folks are home."

Barry doesn't wake but rolls away from me sort of annoyed, saying, "Leave me alone; besides, the door is locked." This doesn't quell my rising panic at all. I just lay there listening to the music. I can't imagine how he could stay asleep with all the noise going on in the house. I hear food frying, music playing, people laughing. Someone is running and talking in the hall and I catch the sounds of an automatic garage door opening outside with a car pulling into it. I search amongst the scattered clothes for my shirt and underwear just in the nick of time because there is a knock on Barry's bedroom door. "Hey Rip! Mom wants you down for breakfast!" I figure it is his older brother. I guess he means RIP as in Rip Van Winkle. Barry doesn't answer. He just rolls over again. The doorknob rattles and turns, which sends me flying out of bed and into an upright position.

"Screw you!" Barry finally calls, causing a loud banging on the other side. Hearing the footsteps walk away from the door and then down the stairs brings me only temporary relief. Maybe I should wake Barry. However, this episode leads me to think that Barry is not a 'morning' person and that I had better let him be. I hear big heavy footsteps coming up the stairs towards us and there is another loud knock.

"Barry, aufwachen!" It's his father. Barry sluggishly gets up with the comforter wrapped loosely around him, and walks towards the door. To my horror, he opens the door and says to his father, "Ein freund schläft bei mir." This is all rather interesting, and puts Barry in a new light. His father mumbles something in German and then Barry replies, "Mark." Upon hearing my name his father immediately switches to English.

"Ah yes, Mark. Good Morning, Mark!" Barry's father offers, pushing the door wider to get a look at me. I feel a red heat come over me.

"Hi, Mr. Stillwater."

"This time you must join us at the table," he replies with his thick accent. I yawn uncontrollably and somehow am able to reply in the positive. Barry looks back at me with a sleepy, happy grin. Barry's father is very tall and handsome. He looks pretty normal, or Canadian, until he speaks. When he is gone Barry closes the door and falls sheepishly on the bed beside me. His hands embrace my legs. "How come you didn't tell me you were from Germany?" I ask. "Because I'm not; my father is," Barry replies. He goes on to say that their real German family name was Stilleswasser and that his dad took on the English translation, Stillwater, when he immigrated to Canada. We eventually get up and throw on our clothes, or rather I throw on my old clothes while Barry puts on a fresh pair of jeans and a t-shirt that are hanging over the chair by his desk. I wet down my hair and borrow Barry's comb. I can only lessen the bad hair day I'm going to have, not stop it. However, I don't use Barry's toothbrush as he offers, causing him to smirk at me with disappointment. I gargle with mouthwash, making my mouth feel a bit fresher. I'm not feeling particularly clean on account of our actions last night. I would have liked to have showered and put on a fresh set of clothes before meeting Barry's family. I figure their first impression of me wasn't exactly a positive one. As we walk downstairs I hear people pulling chairs to sit down at the table.

I whisper to Barry, "Does your mother speak German?"

"Yes, and French" he replies, "My mom grew up in Canada but her family is from Alsace Lorraine." I make a note of this for future investigation because I have no idea where this Alsace place is. Barry's mentioning of his mother brings back fears of my first encounter with her. Upon entering the kitchen my eyes first fall upon Barry's mom. In a way, I'm sort of attracted to her. She looks very much like Barry and much younger than she actually is. She is leaning over the table, placing cartons of milk and orange juice beside her eldest son.

In an effort to win her over, and mustering up all the courage I can, I say, "I'm sorry, I haven't been properly introduced. I'm Mark Thomas." I say it to the room but I am aiming for Barry's mom. "No," she replies coldly, "You did introduce yourself as Sheila's son." It is actually Barry's father who answers. "Yah, Mark, this is my eldest son, Steven, my daughter Lisa, and my wife Helen. We are glad that you decided to join us this time for a meal." Barry's father is trying to make a joke with that last comment, to break the ice, but it doesn't go over with this crowd. Barry just gives his dad a disapproving look as he sits down, grabbing the OJ from his sister. Mrs. Stillwater motions me to sit on the opposite side, away from Barry, which makes me a little paranoid. I feel she suspects something between Barry and me. I get a sense that she does not like me at all. We're served a large and greasy breakfast with ham, scrambled eggs, toast, and fried bratwurst. We quickly and wordlessly pass the food around, just like on the TV show Rosanne. The conversation is light and I do the best I can to join in. I complement Mrs. Stillwater on the meal. She nonchalantly says, "Thank you, Mark. Help yourself to more if you'd like." Mr. Stillwater is the inquisitive one at the table. Steven is sort of a big dopey brother. He is cool but not as composed as Barry. He talks a lot about sports with Barry. At one point, he asks if I am on the basketball team. Barry stops eating and looks up wondering what to do.

"Not this year," I say, to put Barry at ease. The subject quickly changes when Lisa starts talking about her classmates. Lisa is sitting next to me. I think she is more accepting of me, like her father. Steven seems indifferent. It is Mrs. Stillwater who tips the scales against me. I remember Barry telling me how similar he is to his mother, which is not reassuring at this point. I realize then that I hadn't told my mother where I spent the night. In the middle of the meal, I ask if I can use the phone. My sudden action causes everyone to stop what they are doing. Nice move, stupid.

"Sure," answers Mr. Stillwater, still chewing his food. "There's one in the den," Barry adds. He is getting up to take me there when I say that's okay, I'll just use the one on the counter. Big Mistake. Mrs. Stillwater looks disapprovingly at me. It's probably due to the fact that I will be disrupting the conversation at the breakfast table. So, to appease her, I walk myself into the den. I really could have used Barry's help in finding the phone. It was as if he read my mind, because within seconds I hear his footsteps coming up the short stairs behind me, still holding a fork in his hand. He walks past me and picks up the phone, sitting hidden on a small table behind the couch. He hands it to me. I call my mom. I know she'll be home. "Hello?" she answers in her perky sales voice. "Mom, it's me." I tell her that I stayed the night at Barry's and should be home soon. I anticipate a lecture but don't get one. She just says okay and tells me she's running out the door for a showing. This day has been weird from the start. I return to the table. By now, everyone is almost done and they are all clearing the table. I sit alone and finish my meal with all this activity buzzing around me. When I'm done, Barry motions me back upstairs, making me feel awkward on account of our actions last night. Steven and Mr. Stillwater are heading towards the garage and Lisa is in the den with the TV on. Mrs. Stillwater is cleaning up in the kitchen. It all seems like a typical Saturday at the Stillwater house. I follow Barry upstairs and we tidy up around the bedroom. During the course of cleaning, Barry steals a kiss, which makes me panic because the door is open. We go downstairs and out the front door. Barry walks around the side of the house to the garage and reappears with a basketball. He throws it to me and I look around for the hoop, making a shot that falls right in. Barry takes the ball and dribbles with it a bit. I'm not really in the mood to play, and am a little self-conscious of the fact that his father and brother are in the garage doing something. Barry continues to dribble around me like he wants a one-on-one. I stand there, just staring into space. I finally say that I should go. Barry continues to dribble, muttering, "Suit yourself." But

I can tell he is disappointed. He walks me to the end of his driveway. I tell him that I didn't sleep well last night and will probably have a nap when I get home.

"What are you going to do," I inquire. He says he has chores and that he has to go to school to get his jacket and give Monica a call. He realizes his mistake in that last statement.

"Well, I have to say something about my disappearance last night," he retorts angrily. But then says he'll call me, as if to appease me. I nod and walk off feeling mad, confused and tired.

I get home and feel really beat. Taggs comes downstairs and starts jumping all over me. I am far too pooped to even calm him down. I just want to chill for awhile. I walk into the kitchen to find a note on the table.

Mark,

You really should have called to let me know where you were going to be last night. Don't forget to clean the den. Also, could you clean your room? I found it rather untidy.

Love,
Mom

I think it's funny because my room is always a mess, but I guess she feels that if she has to shell out $175 for sneakers, she has a right to make sure they stay in a nice environment. I turn and guzzle some OJ from the fridge and head off to my room. Taggs follows. I should shower first but I am too tired. I drift off to sleep for a couple of hours. Waking up, I still feel drowsy, making the entire past twenty-four hours seem like a blur. It's weird because I have nothing to do, but I want to do something. When I walk downstairs, I see my mother sitting there drinking what looks like a rye and Coke. "Do you always have to stay up in that room?" she slurs, meaning she has had several rye and Cokes. Sometimes I feel like the babysitter between my two parents. I grudgingly walk through the kitchen and open the fridge. I am about to guzzle some orange juice again when I realize that mom is watching in horror. I make a funny face and turn to get a glass. "So, did you deliver the packet to the Stillwater's?" "Yes," I reply with a grin so wide I looked like a Halloween pumpkin.Mom starts to ask about the Stillwater's. I really don't want to get into a deep conversation about them. Mom persists. "So what type of furniture do they have?" I tell her that I don't know. "What do you mean you don't know, is it cheap Ikea crap, or nice Ethan Allen furniture?" Mom gets this way when she is drinking. If I go into another room she'll follow me. If I go out, she'll make a scene at the door. So, I decide it will be best to wait it out and appease her. I describe the furniture as best as I can. Mom sits there listening, as if the words are making her sadder. I am sure she is thinking about her failed marriage, old furniture and her overly demanding career. There is a long silence after I stop talking. She snaps out of her daze as if caught off guard, and goes into a new line of questioning. "So, tell me about the Stillwater kids." With a struggle, I tell her that Barry is their middle child and that I have some classes with him. However, Mom abruptly steers the conversation towards Mr. And Mrs. Stillwater. I sense that mom is envious of Mrs. Stillwater: her looks, her marriage, house and their children. I feel that whatever I'tell her isn't going to be enough. "What does their furniture look like again?" Mom continues.

"I already told you."

"You just don't want to tell your old mother again," she pouts while taking another big gulp from her glass.

"Oh, I don't know, dark stained wood," I reply in desperation. Mom cuts me off by turning on the radio. She is fishing for depressing music, I can tell. She finds a nice Jan Arden song to drown out her sorrows.

"Do you think she's a better mother than me?" Mom murmurs.

"Who?" I ask.

"Mrs. Stillwater" she angrily retorts, as if I should know who she is talking about.

"I don't think so," I honestly reply. This seems to quell the sea of questions. This time when I see a lull in the questioning, I take it as my cue to leave. Mom is staring out the window with a very sad look on her face. I feel kind of guilty about her loneliness. So I do something that I have rarely done in my life. I go over and hug my mom. Her response is so welcoming and strong, as if to say Thank You. I feel awkward.

She suddenly starts to cry and holds me tighter. "Don't cry, you're a great mom," I assure her as I pull away. I go down to the den to play some Xbox. I leave her to her music, cigarettes and booze. She is rocking herself, swaying to the music. She looks so sad it breaks my heart.

CHAPTER EIGHT

The Mark Hall Story

Barry and I are sitting in the library when the story of Mark Hall breaks in the news. Mark Hall is an Oshawa teenager who wanted to take his male date to the prom but was denied by the Principal and Catholic School Board. We are talking about our future university plans. Barry wants to go to a university in the States. Although it isn't said, I suspect that he might have gotten some scholarship offers, due to his basketball skills. I tell Barry that my dream is to go to McGill University in Montreal to eventually study law. Barry doesn't know what he wants to do yet. He is quiet for awhile. When I ask what he is thinking he says nothing, but sighs.

I ask him about his opinion of Mark Hall and the whole situation. Barry doesn't comment on it. I think he is scared that I'm going to ask him to the prom. He only comments that he's certain that if the school board doesn't allow it, Mark will probably take it to court. Just then, Monica and her posse of overly made-up girls in Versace clothing and Max cosmetics walk up and greet Barry. Barry looks up rather nervously, giving me quick glances to see if I'm okay. I am not. However, I have to admit that Barry handles it as best he can. Somehow I feel Monica is flashing me an I-know-What-You-did-Last-Summer look. The thought of it makes me laugh to myself because I actually did nothing last summer but certainly did do something BIG over the weekend.

Sure enough, the following day Mark Hall files a lawsuit that will be destined for the Supreme Court of Canada. Most of the opinions by both my fellow students and faculty are positive and supportive of Mark Hall's situation. Monica starts complaining to everyone how gays want all the attention in this country. Barry gives me the feeling that we aren't allowed to join in on this conversation. When no one participates in the conversation, she turns again to Barry and says loudly, "I had fun on the phone," so that everyone can hear and think that they do it all the time. I can tell it is a desperate plea for recognition from the group that she and Barry have something. Monica touches Barry's collar as she turns to leave. I know that if she would have dared, she would have kissed him, but something in his body position makes it difficult for her to move in. Nice one Barry! I am smiling on the sidelines and determined not to let her get to me. It is mostly a failing effort but still, I keep appearances up for Barry's sake. All the news seems to cover the Mark Hall lawsuit and I feel ashamed that I don't have the courage to be more open about my feelings. I really want to talk to Barry about it but he won't discuss it. He always gives me a short answer and changes the subject. When Barry is at practice, I find my way to our school library computer and start looking up everything I can find on the Mark Hall case. I am so scared that someone might catch me reading it that whenever I hear someone approaching me I quickly minimize the screen.

I decide to stop going to the games and this leaves me with a lot of free time. With Friday here and me home alone, I decide to take Taggs for a walk. However, Taggs is barking at the door as if we have a visitor. Hoping that it will be Barry, I open the door grinning, but the grin quickly disappears. "Hey Kiddo, you stood me up at the basketball game." I had completely forgotten about dad and should have remembered to call him.

"Sorry, I forgot to call. Mom's out showing houses and I was just about to go walk the dog." Dad gladly joins me and remarks that it's been a long time since he's gotten to walk Taggs. As we walk, I start to explain to dad about my plans for university. I tell him as straightforward as I can. I really have no emotional attachment since there are bigger things that I'm addressing in my mind right now. However, dad seems very concerned with how I am coping with friendships, the basketball incident, and life in general. What's sad is that I don't want to talk about these things; what I really want to talk about is Barry. However, I can't bring myself to discuss this topic with him, or anyone else for that matter. But I do the next best thing: I ask him for his thoughts on the Mark Hall trial. Dad seems very knowledgeable about the subject since it's been playing every day for the past week on the news. He feels that sexuality is a personal journey and that in today's society gays want more rights and that he is okay with this issue. "If Mark Hall was your son, would you let him sue the government?" I ask. "Heck, I'd pay for the suit myself," he spouts out with pride. I almost want to tell him about Barry but I am just happy to know my dad will have an open mind towards a gay son. I really feel Mark Hall has great courage, whereas Barry and I do not.Dad and I walk and talk for nearly an hour. I guess it makes him feel good to "bond" with me. He tries his best to be supportive and I'm glad he's concerned. But then I make the mistake of asking my father, "How did he know he was in love?" He looks at me with a peculiar smile and starts to tell me his theory of love. According to dad, love is what you're willing to do for a person. "You know your mother and I," then he pauses. "Well, I thought she was it for me, but you know Mark, you can love again." Isn't that a song? I will love again? I laugh and my dad playfully grabs me and laughs along.I only see his second wife and my half sister on holidays and special events. I know that it's polite to ask about them and so I do. Dad seems to take pleasure in filling me in on their day-to-day activities. I think he feels the need to fill me in on them just in case I will be stepping into their family unit soon. I always find it awkward that my father has two lives. I know it's quite common and I don't know why it bothers me so much. We have never really talked about the divorce or my feelings about it.

It is dark by the time we get to the house. The lights are on and mom's car is in the driveway. Dad comes in with me. Although the divorce was amicable, I can still sense a bit of tension between my parents. I think my mom is resentful that my father remarried so quickly. They exchange hellos and dad inquires about mom's work. He is always careful not to talk about his new life, and mom's always careful not to ask. Dad leaves shortly after and mom becomes quiet.

It is late in March that the University acceptance letters start coming in. I will happily tell Barry which schools are accepting me. I am pleased to see that I get into both Dalhousie and McGill. Mom is leaning towards McGill and dad towards Dalhousie, because he's from Halifax originally and it's his alma mater. It might be good to get in touch with my family roots back there.

CHAPTER NINE

Rave Party

S pring is here and when we don't have heavy school obligations, Barry and I spend almost all of our waking moments together. In private, I spend all my time reading any stories I can find about the Mark Hall trial. Barry and I really enjoy each other's company. We can just sit around all day and listen to music. Or, we'll lie on our backs on his bed and watch the clouds out the window and say nothing. We venture out into the city sometimes. One night we go to a rave party. It is only by chance that we see a crumpled flyer on the floor at the Oakville Mall advertising the underground rave. It only catches my eye because of the rainbow flag. It is to be held off Queen Street West in Toronto. "Sixty dollars," I yell, pointing at the admission price. Barry shrugs. "I don't have $60. I will barely have enough for the fare to get to

Toronto and back," I tell him. "Well, how much can you raise?" Barry asks. "I don't know, forty bucks at best," I muse, deep in thought. "Look, give me the $40 and don't worry about the rest." Barry offers. We have both heard about raves before, but never gay ones. Barry looks at me and wonders aloud if we should check it out. We plot our escape to the city with ease. We pack overnight bags for our big trip into Toronto. We lie to our parents, telling them we are sleeping over at each other's houses. We take the Go Train at 10:57 p.m., arriving in Toronto at 12:30 a.m. We are the only two people in the Go Train car. We are both filled with nervous energy and feeling jumpy. Everything seems so big and scary in Toronto at night. When we arrive in Toronto, we soon realize that we have no idea where this place is located. Barry hails a cab from Union Station to the address on Queen Street West. It is just off Queen Street down a dingy lane flanked by rows of old warehouses. It is obvious from the flashing lights which building is holding the rave. When the cab stops and Barry goes to pay the fair, Barry pulls out a massive wad of cash. I have never seen so much money in my life. He quickly pays the driver and stuffs the rest into his pants pocket, making a big bulge in his jeans. We are standing in the entrance line-up. The clothes some of the others are wearing are outlandish. We look so plain in comparison to everyone else. Guys in dresses, guys in feather boas and underwear, muscle T-shirts, and glitter everywhere. I know Barry is not going to like this but so far he seems okay with it. The building is an abandoned red brick warehouse of some sort. There are windows with missing window panes. The broken pavement in the alleyway has sections missing and dead grass patches everywhere. I guess there are about 100 people in the line-up but it is moving quickly. There are two hot Spanish guys ahead of us. They each keep talking into their cell phones in Spanish very loudly the entire time they are in the line-up. I think that is rude because it would have been nice to at least have had the chance to talk to them. I have never seen so many gay men together in one group, ever. I am excited and I want to make friends. The lineup is too long so they switch to randomly checking. We get in without being checked. We were prepared to get rejected right away, but it doesn't happen.

Inside, there are hundreds of people crammed together, and blaring music and laser lights flashing and waving everywhere. The echo from the high ceiling makes the music take on an odd effect. The heat radiating from the dance floor feels great. The whole vibe is exhilarating.

Barry and I weave our way through the crowd and go right to the bar and order drinks for ourselves. I think drinking might be the only way Barry can deal with this craziness. He has all the money; I gave him my $40 as he promised to cover the rest. I know he has a lot of money but I had no idea how much. I see him quickly chug down his rum and Coke and look around nervously; he orders another before I even get to sip mine. This is a side of Barry that I don't know about. I nurse my drink because I am not really much of a drinker. As the alcohol sets in, Barry is getting touchy-feely with me. He seems more relaxed and able to laugh more.

The music, although blaringly loud, has a good beat to it. Guys are bumping and grinding everywhere. There are even guys kissing each other on the dance floor. I want to dance, and Barry obliges me. This is the first time Barry and I dance together. It seems both awkward and cool at the same time. Barry doesn't mind much because he is already drunk. He keeps coming up to me to grind, and it makes me laugh and I push him away. Barry, being drunk, takes it as a game and makes silly bull horns with his fingers as he comes at me again. Guys are dancing, kissing and grinding all around us. It makes me feel overjoyed. As my inhibitions lower, I kiss Barry on the dance floor. Our kiss is really passionate and lasts a long time. No one cares. This is great. I can smell the rum on his breath. We dance for awhile and are both pretty drenched with sweat by the time we get back to the bar. Barry goes to order but I interject, "Water for both of us please." Barry frowns at my insistence but nods in confirmation to the bartender. I don't like this side of Barry. It is new to me and I conclude it makes him seem more human. I don't think that I'm losing interest in Barry, but I have now had time to understand him better, recognizing some of his weaknesses, or faults. I know no one is perfect, but he seems to be a follower. I feel that I have more guts to stand up for what I believe in, in my own way, than he does. However, this recklessness in getting drunk makes me think how immature he can be at times.

We get our waters and Barry motions that he has to go to the restroom. I follow him, but this doesn't seem to bother him. Barry goes into the only free cubicle. As he finishes his business, I hear one of the cubicle doors bang open. A tall muscular man walks out, zipping up his fly and leaving a girl behind. The cubicle door is obviously still open and there, sitting on the toilet with her underwear round her ankles, is a slim, redheaded girl. I peer in but I can't see her face as she is hiding her head in her hands.

"Are you alright?" I ask her. She lifts her head up and tries to focus. I guess she has had quite a bit to drink. By now Barry has joined me.

Not being one for subtlety, I ask, "Did that guy rape you?" This makes Barry look at me like I am from another planet. She shakes her head. "Should I get help? Are you alright?" I ask again, trying desperately to cover up my stupidity.

"Will you stop with the questions?" she snaps. "I have no idea who that guy was. I just dragged him in here for some fun, okay?"

"Okay." Barry agrees, slightly annoyed and taken aback. "We'll leave you alone then."

"No, please don't go." she pleads. "I think I'm going to puke."

"Pull up your pants and then we'll help you," I say. She does this and tries to stand. We quickly see that she is not very steady on her feet, but then again, neither is Barry at this point. I have to reach out to stop her from falling backwards, and manage to grab her purse before it falls into the toilet. They stagger over to the sinks where she immediately starts throwing up.

"Thanks," she says as Barry hands her a paper towel to wipe her mouth. "You are quite the boy scout!"

"It's the least I can do," he replies. The girl smiles and grabs for Barry's crotch. "Whoa, I'm not sure that's a good idea," Barry laughs. "I'm with someone."

"This cutie here?" She turns to grab at me and almost loses her balance.

"I'm Mark," I say, trying to be friendly although I'm mildly freaked out by this chick who's drunk, in the men's bathroom at a gay rave, and looking to have sex with my boyfriend. Guys are passing us by on their way to the stalls, not paying any attention to us.

"Kara," she replies. "Mind if I borrow your boyfriend?" She's trying to get Barry to kiss her, but with no success. I pull her away but Barry makes the matter worse by trying to kiss me. This is a messy situation here and I am the only sober one. The problem is what to do with Kara. Kara is very pretty, and a few years older than us. I look at my watch. It's 5 a.m.

"Should we take her home?" I ask Barry. "Yes," Kara answers, grinning at Barry. I tell her we don't live here but we could drop her off. I tell her it's our first rave. Kara's face breaks into a grin. "Aw, how old are you guys? You look so adorable." Barry gets a panicked look on his face, thinking I am going to blow our cover. Instead, I motion her towards the door where all three of us stumble our way to the exit. Fortunately, there are cabs waiting and we're able to catch one. We all pile inside and I ask Kara for her address. "Robinson and Bathurst, 2355 Robinson Street near Bathurst." The cabbie drives off. Thankfully, it isn't very far. Barry insists we take her up to her suite as it looks like she has passed out. Kara, upon waking, agrees and invites us up. It is chilly as our sweat has now dried and our cold, damp clothing presses against our bodies. We clamber up the cement steps and Kara rifles through her purse for the keys. I figure it will take her forever to open the door, so I insist on unlocking it for her. I search for the light switch, fumble and find one. The light is a florescent fixture that makes everything look putrid yellow. Before us is a steep set of stairs which take forever to get a half-sleeping Kara and a staggering Barry up. I turn on another light switch and see a living room area in front of me where I can put Kara down safely. I slump her onto a beanie bag that sits in the center of the room. A black and white cat comes in meowing at all the commotion. I go down the hallway to find the kitchen and Barry follows me. He is clinging to me and wants to kiss again. I am not in the mood for this but appreciate the gesture. He pouts but quickly changes his mind when we find the kitchen. I locate a pot and boil some water for tea. I find the tea bags in the cupboard. Barry keeps snooping through drawers, making a lot of noise. "Do you want some tea?" I ask him. He shakes his head as he opens the fridge and pulls out a Brita water filter and asks for water instead. I give him a mug from a matching set on the counter. I bring two mugs of hot tea into the living room and give one to Kara. She is somewhat awake now. We flop on the chesterfield in front of the television set next to her.

"You guys a couple?" We both look at each other and smile. "Yes," we say in unison, laughing at our random answer. "Awww, that's so sweet. Sorry, I tried to do it with you there, what's your name?" "Barry," he replies, smiling. I like Kara even though she was acting like a total whore at the rave. She is the first person to know our secret. We tell her about ourselves and she speaks about herself. She's a receptionist for a mutual fund company. All the time we are chatting, Barry and I are holding hands. It is sun up when the conversation breaks off and sleep overtakes us. She shows us where some blankets are and we crash on her living room floor while she sleeps in her bed.

She is still sound asleep when Barry and I wake up. I hate to admit it, but we fooled around while she was sleeping in the next room. When Barry and I are fully awake, Kara doesn't seem to want to get up. So we leave her to her sleep. I fish around in a desk drawer for a pen and paper and leave her a note thanking her for her hospitality. I give her my email address and hope to hear from her. We catch a cab at the corner and it takes us to Union Station.

Barry is hung over during the train ride, but trying to hide it. The ride home is in utter silence. We don't reach our respective homes until 4:30 p.m. on Sunday.

I feel so dirty and tired. I shower and watch some TV before going to bed.

CHAPTER TEN

After High School

Most of all, Barry loves the long walks with Taggs in the ravine. Barry will often show up with treats and canned dog food for Taggs. Mom, in some way, thinks that our friendship has evolved around Taggs and Barry's need for canine companionship. It pleases me to see mom so off the mark with her opinion. It is during one of our long walks when Barry brings up what I knew was going to happen anyway. "I have to tell you something," Barry nervously blurts out. "I am going to the prom with Monica." He quickly glances over at me to see my reaction. I have a hollow knot in my stomach and I want to ask why, but I can't find the words.

"Well, I guess I will have to trust you," I say softly. We walk the remaining time in silence. Taggs trots along unaware of the conversation that has just transpired. We say our goodbyes. The air between us is so thick I can hardly breathe. My head has so many thoughts banging around inside that I am getting a headache. I wonder if Barry took me to the rave because he knew he had to deliver this bad news to me.

Barry had no intention of inviting me to the prom. Barry is not Mark Hall. In a way, Mark Hall becomes my hero out of Barry's failure to make things right. It is Monica who breaks the story to the group that she and Barry will be going together.

On prom night, all the boys book a room at the hotel. They dress as if they are going stag. They rent limos and pick up their dates at their homes. Barry buys Monica a white corsage. At Monica's house pictures are taken to capture the memories. This all transpires just a few hundred yards from where I am sitting, watching television alone.Neither my mother nor my father asks if I am going to the prom. I watch TV until I get bored with it and then I trudge up the stairs with Taggs trailing behind me. I am pretty numb. I don't want to think about the meaning of this day. Just as I suspect, it is a pretty uneventful prom. Barry and Monica hang out a bit. They dance and they kiss, but I think Barry lets it be known that there is someone else on his mind.The day after the prom, Barry comes over to hang out with me, but it is the day that I had set aside to spend with my dad. I am really surprised to see both of them in the foyer when I come downstairs. There is a bit of an awkward silence among us. I make the introductions. Dad offers to take both Barry and me out for lunch and, oddly, they both wait for my response, instead of Barry answering. So we take Barry to Kelsey's, our family's usual spot. Barry seems eager to talk with my father. I can't remember Barry ever being so talkative and forward before. My dad is equally friendly, and I know this will mean that I'll have to sit through embarrassing "when Mark was a kid" stories. As we are seated, Todd Polino and Judy Aronson come over to our table. They make small talk about the prom with Barry, practically disregarding my father and me. My father gazes over at me, giving me a puzzled look. When Todd and Judy leave, my dad asks Barry if he went to the prom. Barry answers, looking ashamed. A moment of silence falls upon the table. My father senses the tension and is able to put it all together. He looks at us and says, "We don't all have to be Mark Halls." Barry shoots me a nervous look and I have no idea where my father is going with this, but fortunately, the server comes to take our orders and saves us. Soon the conversation turns along the lines of future plans, basketball, families, and more "when Mark was little" stories. Dad really goes out of his way to bond with Barry, and it seems to be working. I never saw Barry so at ease with an adult before, and it's then more than ever that I realize my dad is a pretty amazing guy. When lunch is over and dad is dropping us off, I reach over and hug him hard and he hugs me back. "You know I love you son, no matter what" It's enough to make me cry but I hold back in front of Barry. I've done enough of that already.

As my dad drives off, Barry and I watch his car disappear as it turns off our street. "Your dad is a really great guy. You never told me that he was like that." The next morning, Barry is at my door asking to take Taggs for a walk. I leave Barry to play with Taggs while I shower. Mom is out showing homes and we have the whole house to ourselves. When I come down, we both look at each other, getting intimate ideas. However, I move for the door as if to say that we should really walk the dog. We take our usual path.

I tell him that I read in the news that Mark Hall and his boyfriend, Jean-Paul Dumond, have broken up. I think they still went to the prom together. Barry nods in acknowledgement but his thoughts are elsewhere. "I have to go to Germany for the summer," Barry tells me. His parents want to spend the summer with their German relatives. Barry looks at me and tells me that he wants to give me something special, to make it right. He reaches into his pocket and presents me with his acceptance letter from McGill.

I am really growing up fast, and now university doesn't seem such a long time away.

The End

The Gay Icon Contemporary Short Stories
by Robert Joseph Greene
(ISBN 9780986929762)

This collection of Icon Contemporary Short Stories is a series of male experiences to varying degrees of depth. It looks at the gay experience with modern day living for most of us and it connects us with a certain understanding of the human heart. Please note, that some of these stories are in other eBook collections. Table of Contents: 1) Introduction 2) The Difference Between Buddies And Lovers 3) The Stones On The Floor 4) The E-Mail Message 5) The Measure Of Love 6) Oh Shit 7) The Abyss 8) The Understanding 9) Earl's Child 10) The Wrong Voice Far Away 11) The Thin Line

The Gay Icon Classics Of The World
by Robert Joseph Greene
(ISBN 9780986929755)

A wonderful collection of gay short fiction fables from around the world. The creation of these stories were based upon some cultural awareness of gay men in history and in some cultures where gay life is taboo. This is a must read for people who are interested in gaining an understanding of gays from different cultures and the human heart. Table of Contents 1. Introduction 2. The Journey and the Jewels – Saudi Arabia 3. And Cupid Also Loved – Rome 4. Haakon of Hearts – Sweden 5. The Wrong Voice Far Away – Egypt 6. Bantu's Song and the Soiled Loin Cloth – Côte d'Ivoire 7. The Five Bows of Shakespeare's Apprentice – Great Britain 8. The Three Wishes – Mexico 9. The Barton – France 10. The Love of Falleron and Ibsen – Greece 11. Halo's Golden Circle – Judea (Israel)